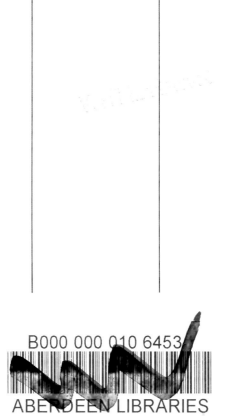

ABERDEEN
CITY LIBRARIES

All aboard for some seasonal magic on

The Christmas Express!

These gorgeous docs never expected to
find love...especially in time for Christmas!
During a magical train journey on the opulent
Orient Express, from romantic Venice to
cosmopolitan London, their ride of a lifetime
brings lifesaving drama and the chance for
their hearts to be finally unlocked!

FROM VENICE WITH LOVE
by Alison Roberts

CHRISTMAS WITH HER EX
by Fiona McArthur

Dear Reader

Who can resist the romance and glitz of the world's most glamorous train journey? Certainly not Alison Roberts and I. So we travelled in *olde world* style from Venice to London on the famous Orient Express, always with the idea that we would write these books.

And what a magical journey it was. From the canals of Venice to the soaring Italian Dolomites, crossing snow-covered valleys and burrowing through the mountains of the Austrian Alps, with men in tuxedos and women in sequins... It's a journey we will never forget.

I'd love you to share the journey with my heroine, Kelsie Summers, an independent midwife who has always dreamed she'd ride this train one day, and Connor Black, the man she left outside the register office fifteen years ago.

Offering his seat to Kelsie in Venice two days before Christmas is bad, but leaving her alone with his meddling grandmother is a hundred times worse. Connor can't believe his bad luck, or the surge of emotion as he looks at the woman he crossed a world to get away from after she broke his heart.

Through the next thirty-six hours and into the night the train blazes a trail across the countryside, past the bells of railway crossings and the flashes of light, while its occupants sleep in their little beds until dawn outside Paris. Such fabulous fun as Kelsie and Connor rediscover and then lose each other again while the train shoots through the tunnel to England and the white cliffs of Dover, past keeps and stone walls and English backyards, until it reaches the bustle of London and the magic of Christmas.

I wish you a happy journey!

Fiona xxx

CHRISTMAS WITH HER EX

BY
FIONA McARTHUR

First published in Great Britain 2013
by Mills & Boon, an imprint of Harlequin (UK) Limited.
Harlequin (UK) Limited, Eton House, 18-24 Paradise Road, Richmond, Surrey TW9 1SR

© Fiona McArthur 2013

ISBN: 978 0 263 23388 9

Harlequin (UK) policy is to use papers that are natural, renewable and recyclable products and made from wood grown in sustainable forests. The logging and manufacturing process conform to the legal environmental regulations of the country of origin.

Printed and bound in Great Britain
by CPI Antony Rowe, Chippenham, Wiltshire

Mother to five sons, **Fiona McArthur** is an Australian midwife who loves to write. Mills & Boon® Medical Romance™ gives Fiona the scope to write about all the wonderful aspects of adventure, romance, medicine and midwifery that she feels so passionate about—as well as an excuse to travel! Now that her boys are older, Fiona and her husband, Ian, are off to meet new people, see new places, and have wonderful adventures. Fiona's website is at www.fionamcarthur.com

Also by Fiona McArthur:

These books are also available in eBook format from www.millsandboon.co.uk

For my darling husband,
who watched our travels via internet banking,
with words of caution and judicious injections of
funds, and the fuzzy but fabulous use of Skype.

Praise for
Fiona McArthur:

'McArthur does full justice to an intensely emotional
scene of the delivery of a stillborn baby—
one that marks a turning point in both the characters'
outlooks. The entire story is liberally spiced with
drama, heartfelt emotion and just a touch of humour.'
—*RT Book Reviews* on
SURVIVAL GUIDE TO DATING YOUR BOSS

'MIDWIFE IN A MILLION by Fiona McArthur
will leave readers full of exhilaration.
Ms McArthur has created characters
that any reader could fall in love with.'
—*Cataromance*

PROLOGUE

THE SEAGULLS WERE screaming—or maybe it was him. Twelve-year-old Connor saw the wave lift his mother and tumble her over and over.

He was running but it was too late.

He should have told her not to go back. The words had been on his lips.

He should never have held them back.

'A quick look for Daddy's ring,' she'd said. 'I must have dropped it in the rock pool.'

But he'd known the tide was coming in. The last wave had made them run from the rocks. And now...

'Look after your mother,' Dad had said, and he hadn't. He should have said, *No! Dont go. The waves are too big. They'll sweep you out. You don't have time.*

The wave... And then another...

And then there were people—shouting, helping. Reaching his mother as he couldn't. They'd get her.

But, no. A man was carrying his mother towards the sand, and his mother was limp like the seaweed that washed this way and that in the waves.

Her long hair was touching the sand as they came closer. He saw her face—and he knew nothing would ever be the same.

He knew he should have stopped her. He knew it. *He knew it.* Now…the way she was lying.…he knew something awful had happened.

He'd disobeyed his father. His mother was dying and he knew it was his fault.

CHAPTER ONE

As Kelsie Summers floated in her gondola past St Mark's Square she thought of last night's Christmas-themed mass at St Mark's Cathedral and she rubbed the goose-bumps on her arms at the memory it evoked. The strings of Christmas fairy lights over the Bridge of Sighs had winked last night and now, though extinguished, they still decorated the canals and bridges of Venice on her way to the station.

Her bag was full of nativity scenes in glass and gorgeous Christmas-tree globes for her friends.

Even the crumbling mansions on the Venice waterways had gorgeous glass mangers and angels in their lower windows and she watched the last of them fade into the distance as her gondolier ducked under the final bridge.

The end of two weeks of magic and her trip of a lifetime—and so what if she'd originally planned to share it with someone long gone, she'd still made it happen.

The bow of the long black boat kissed the wharf and the gondolier swung Kelsie's bag up onto the narrow boardwalk the same way as he held the craft steady, with little effort. She'd chosen the strongest-looking gondolier for just that reason.

She stepped out, in not very sensible shoes but she was a little more dressed up than usual in honour of the coming journey, and then her tasselled-hatted hero abandoned her cheerfully as he pushed off.

Kelsie dragged her bag up the planking to solid ground, or as solid as she could get in Venice, and sniffed away the idea of tears.

Surely she wasn't weepy just because of the lack of gentlemen to help her move this huge bag! It was because she was leaving Venice. Because her lifelong travel dream was coming to an end.

Modern-day women didn't need male help, Kelsie told herself, but the Stazione di Venezia, and the Santa Lucia steps, mocked her as she glanced down with a grimace.

A passing Venetian 'gentleman' flicked his nicotine-stained finger at the tiny alley that ran up the side of the building for those who didn't want to hump their belongings up the steps and she smiled her thanks. Bless the inventor of suitcase spinner wheels, and her sense of independence was appeased.

She'd arrived in Venice in a blaze of anticipation via the front entrance to the railway station and it seemed fitting, she wasn't sure why, to be slipping home to the real world of work and her solitary flat more than ten thousand miles away in Sydney, out the back way.

Though once she'd dragged this bulging brick of a suitcase inside, the train she was about to board was anything but the back way, and she felt her spirits soar again.

The last part of her journey—the one she'd dreamt of since a long-ago friend had mentioned his English grandmother embarked on it every year—had captured her imagination while she'd still been in school uniform. Venice to London via the Orient Express—the world's most glamorous train journey. And she'd finally made it happen.

Which was why she was wearing her second-highest heels and her new cream Italian suit. Maybe not so glamorous doing it by yourself, she conceded, but still very glam, and stiffened her spine as she entered the cavernous world of departure beside a tourist shop adorned with miniature gondoliers' hats.

Platform One. She'd entered at the correct platform, arrived at the specified time, so where was the blue and gold emblazoned wagon of the Orient Express?

Kelsie glanced around. Remembered the inside of Saint Lucia from arrival—like any other railway station—grey concrete, cold underfoot, traveller-filled bench seats, matching-luggage families huddled together. Finally she saw a small white sign, very ordinary, very unostentatious, that read 'Meeting Point for Venice Simplon Orient Express'.

Connor Black watched the shoulders of the smartly dressed woman sag as she peered under her dark cap of hair with the perplexed countenance of the unseasoned traveller as she turned her back to him. Her head dipped down at what must be a horrendously heavy suitcase. It was almost bigger than she was, and he wondered if she'd dare try and perch on top of it.

He sighed and stood to offer his seat, brushing away the niggling feeling that he knew her. Of course he didn't. He was in Venice. And if he didn't offer her his

seat Gran would poke him with her silver-topped cane
as if he were a six-year-old until he did. Gran was his
one big weakness and the only woman he loved. Unfortunately she knew it.

He caught his gran's eye as she nodded approvingly
and bit back a grin. Despite her age she looked like a
million pounds in her pink jacket and skirt with her
snow-white hair fresh from her Venetian stylist. The
pink Kimberley diamonds at her wrist and throat glit-
tered under the electric lights. Lord, he would miss the
old minx when she was gone. Had to be the reason he
was standing here in the first place.

He had very special clients, the Wilsons, a couple
he'd worked with for years, whose tenuous assisted
pregnancy had been particularly challenging, and they
were all on tenterhooks until Connie Wilson had this
baby safely delivered. He'd promised her influential
husband, and more importantly the nervous Connie,
he'd be available twenty-four seven.

So he should be somewhere closer to them, instead
of sitting on a train for the next thirty-six hours playing nursemaid to an eighty-year-old lady who should
be at home, knitting. But then even he laughed at the
idea of Gran doing anything of the sort.

The original *grande dame* inclined her eyes sideways
towards the woman several times and he settled her with
his nod. And he'd better be quick about it.

Not used to taking orders from anyone, Connor decided this could prove to be a very long thirty-six hours
as he stepped closer to the woman and spoke from behind her. 'Excuse me. Would you like my seat, madam?'

The woman turned, their eyes met, and recognition slammed him harder than being hit with a suit-case twice the size of hers. Sky-blue eyes. Snub nose. That mouth. The one it had taken him, admittedly in his callow youth, two years to banish from his mind. A face that seemed outlined with a dark crayon line in-stead of the blur every other face was.

Fifteen years ago. Kelsie Summers.

'Or perhaps you'd rather stand.' Luckily that was under his breath because his grandmother's eagle eye had spotted his reaction.

Stunned blue eyes stared frozenly back at his. He saw the movement in her alabaster throat as she swal-lowed, and then her tongue peeped out. Yes, you damn well should lick your lips in consternation, he thought savagely, when you left me at the registry office, cool-ing my heels.

He gestured to the seat beside his grandmother with all the reluctant invitation of a toddler giving away his last lollypop.

Damn if he didn't feel like sitting down again and turning his own back. But that would be childish and he hadn't indulged in such weakness for a long, long, time.

Stinking bad luck, though, to meet her here, and if he knew his grandmother it would be the perfect diver-sion for the boredom that, despite her assurances, would ultimately descend on her before they reached London.

Kelsie felt like sinking into the grey concrete, maybe even through that and into the murky bottom of the Ven-ice waterways that were probably somewhere under the railway station.

This was the first time she'd seen Connor since the day she'd run away.

She'd written, trying to explain why she thought she'd ultimately ruin his life if she married him, sent the tear-streaked missive, had watched from around a corner as he'd paced in agitation waiting for her to arrive, committed every line of his worried face to memory because she'd never see him again.

Though one glance at his face this morning when he'd recognised her and she could tell there still might be something he wanted to say to her about all that. As time had gone on she'd had a little more insight into how he might have felt. She swallowed nervously.

Fifteen years ago, as a teenager, she'd wanted to expect more from herself, too, had wanted her own career, and even then she'd had a core of sense and clarity that the more romantic Connor had lacked. She had wanted to be a wife who brought more to the table than hero-worship.

She'd seen, through eyes that had seen it before between her mother and father, that her deference and his growing tendency to take control might just bring more than order to her sometimes scattered life.

Connor would always be her hero, but as the wedding date had grown closer, slowly it had sunk in further that she hadn't wanted to rely on Connor all her life. She'd wanted to be a woman her husband could be proud of and she wouldn't have been able to do that under his very protective wing.

Well, they were adults now. He'd morphed into a gorgeously handsome hunk with just a touch of silver at his temples—where had those years gone? she wondered in awe. He certainly wasn't nineteen any more, and they'd been far too young to elope anyway. Everyone had told her that. She was also a very different woman now, she thought as he gestured her, less than graciously, to his seat.

'Thank you,' Kelsie said. Not much else she could do. He didn't answer as she sat down, just looked at the older lady in the gorgeous pink designer suit next to her and raised a mocking eyebrow. 'I'm having coffee. Would you like me to get two, Gran?'

'Three.' The older lady turned a sweet smile her way. 'Do you take sugar?'

Kelsie blushed when she realised the woman's intent. No. No. He wouldn't want to buy her coffee, and when she glanced at Connor his smile had such a bitter sardonic tilt to it she lifted her chin. 'White, no sugar. Thank you.'

Connor couldn't believe his stupidity. He'd just wanted to walk away, get his head together—not that he wasn't over her, good grief it had been years ago, but it had been a shock—and coffee had seemed a good excuse. Of course, now the conversation was open there would be no stopping Gran from pumping Kelsie. Her name echoed in his brain and travelled through his body and stirred every nook and cranny into alertness. He shook his head to be rid of it and sighed. Gran would burrow for all the information she could get.

If he'd stayed around and damped down the friendliness, instead of sloping off, he might have been able to hustle Gran onto the train and only bad luck would have made them meet again.

Too little, too late, too bad, and he'd just have to move on, he thought as he picked up the pace and clenched his fist in his pocket. Now he really needed the coffee to wash away the bitterness at the back of his throat.

Funny how feelings he'd thought he'd forgotten rolled in his belly like it was yesterday, and he searched for the anger that had finally obliterated the hurt of her no-show at their wedding. The one person he'd thought he could trust. Damn her.

The forgotten embers flared and the heat of it gave him pause. The rational person he was now frowned it down and locked it away. Douse it. It was water under the bridge, and there were plenty of bridges in Venice to let it wash away, quite symbolic really.

It was just the shock. Not a huge deal after all. He began to feel better.

Sitting uncomfortably on a seat she didn't want, Kelsie watched Connor Black stride away, the man who used to be her best friend, so tall, so rigidly straight, waves of disdain emanating from him like mist from the canals, and she remembered the last time she'd seen him. She hadn't expected it would be fifteen years before she saw him again.

The elderly lady next to her leaned closer and the serene scent of Arpège perfume drifted across the seat. Kelsie inhaled it with a pang and the penny dropped that this must be the woman who rode the Orient Express whom Connor had talked about all those years ago. The reason Kelsie had sketched in this journey on her bucket list.

The elderly lady twinkled up at her, her faded blue eyes shone, brightly inquisitive, and despite the pit that had just opened Kelsie couldn't help a small smile back.

'I'm Winsome Black. And if I'm not mistaken, you know my grandson, Connor?'

'Kelsie Summers. I knew him a long time ago.' She sighed for the idealism of a young Connor and her part in fracturing it.

Winsome snorted. 'Must have been memorable because I rarely see any expression cross my grandson's face and that was a positive grimace.'

'Gee, thanks.' Kelsie couldn't help the rueful smile that escaped. True, it hadn't been a happy face on poor Connor, and she couldn't help another swift peek to where extraordinarily broad shoulders were just disappearing into the station coffee shop.

He'd changed. A lot. She blinked the last image away. He'd always been a favourite with the girls but she'd bet his wife hated having him out of her sight. Where would they be now if she hadn't run away?

'So you're that Kelsie!' It wasn't a question. 'How fascinating.' This was accompanied by a demure smile and an even brighter twinkle in the eye of the older lady, and Kelsie almost wished she'd followed Connor. Her thoughts must have shown because Winsome touched her arm.

'Don't go. I'll be good. But it's Christmas in two days. You could humour an old lady's curiosity just a little.' Not waiting for permission, Winsome launched into her cross-examination. 'Are you married?'

Not a lot she could do about this, Kelsie thought as she accepted the inevitable, so she settled back for the interrogation with what composure she could muster. 'No.'

'Why not? A young, attractive woman like yourself must have had her chances.'

Kelsie shrugged. 'I didn't marry the man I did love. So I wasn't going to marry one I didn't.'

Winsome looked dubious. 'I think that makes sense.'

'And I love my independence and my work.' She hadn't meant to sound defensive. She wasn't feeling defensive!

'I know someone like that.' Winsome shook her head at a thought she didn't share. 'So you're not even engaged?' Inquisitive faded blue eyes twinkled at her again.

Kelsie lifted her chin. 'No.' Her life was good just as it was.

Winsome sat back. 'Connor's not married either.' She acknowledged Kelsie's narrowed gaze and obviously decided she'd pried enough. 'I'll stop.'

Kelsie raised her brows. 'You seemed to have acquired the salient information.' And imparted a bit as well. Why wasn't Connor married?

'My *modus operandi*, dear.'

'I consider myself warned,' Kelsie muttered to herself, but there was food for thought in her new knowledge. How could that be?

As if she'd heard the thought, Winsome added, 'He's been very busy with his career.' Then she smiled and Kelsie wasn't so sure she trusted the unholy glee in the older woman's face. 'And here he comes.'

When Connor arrived he handed Kelsie her coffee without a glance and ignored her murmured thanks.

Winsome accepted hers with all-seeing eyes and directed her attention to her grandson and pretended to sigh. 'I'm disappointed with the waiting room for the world's most glamorous journey.' There was a special twinkle in her eyes as if she knew a secret no one else did.

Connor glanced at the tiny white sign alone on the concrete. 'Me, too. If only I could make it happen for you, Gran, I would.' He snapped his fingers.

As if conjured up, like Mary Poppins's sister, a young woman in a gold-edged royal-blue skirt and high-collared jacket high-heeled her way across the concourse towards them, pushing a tall wooden reception desk on wheels. Another equally well-dressed young woman pushed a covered luggage trolley.

Kelsie blinked. It wasn't luggage on the trolley. It was furniture.

The hostess directed her junior to unroll a plush, deep red carpet stamped with a blue and gold insignia and then...magic.

Kelsie blinked again as within seconds a large circular waiting area sprang up in an empty space on the grey concrete. The beautiful oak reception desk, also sporting insignias, two potted palms in four-legged oak pots, also on wheels, a gold-edged name plate on the desk and a bowl of roses. Kelsie thought they looked suspiciously real.

The young hostess snapped open a box of labels and turned to the bemused crowd. 'Who is first?' She smiled and then disappeared from view for a moment behind the surge of patrons.

'I can see why you travel with him,' Kelsie whispered to Winsome as they stayed seated to allow the crowd to thin, and Winsome nodded complacently.

At that moment the unmistakable sound of a diesel engine and rattle of wheels on rails heralded the arrival of the world's most famous train and everyone paused to look.

Shiny blue carriages, with burnished gold edges and gold lettering, and gleaming panes of glass all came closer until the brakes screeched as the wheels locked on the rails and inched to a stop.

The anticipation in the air rose like the smell of diesel from the train.

Thank goodness for the distraction, Kelsie thought with relief. It was the perfect excuse to put some distance between her and Connor. She turned to Winsome. 'May I leave my bag here while I go and have a closer look?'

Winsome patted her leg. 'Of course.'

Kelsie stood hastily and without glancing at the man looming over her she carried her disposable coffee cup to the platform and began to wander up the length of the train.

Such shiny gold trim around the windows and gorgeous lettering proclaiming 'Express Eurpeen' above the glass, but it was that chance to peer in, that glimpse into a bygone era that attracted her. Each cabin held an ornate bench seat with tiny lace-covered tables and a dainty pink lamp next to a delicate orchid that danced in a slender crystal vase, and everywhere rich, dark panelling glowed in the dim light with exquisite parquetry. She couldn't wait to see which tiny cabin was hers.

Not to mention the relief of being able to hide her face from the steely glance of the man she'd jilted more than a decade ago.

Back on the bench Winsome Black raised her brows quizzically. 'She's very striking.'

'Hmm.' Connor didn't want to think about Kelsie Summers and he certainly didn't want to talk about her. He tried not to glance up the platform but his gaze strayed disobediently before he whipped it back. She still had the whippet thinness he remembered but had gained subtle womanly curves that beckoned anyone with a spoonful of testosterone without her even trying. Typical.

He snapped his teeth together. 'If you give me your ticket I'll check your baggage in. I imagine it will take a while before all these people are checked in and the luggage loaded.'

His grandmother had declined to allow him to care for the tickets. He wasn't used to it. The whole 'not being in command' thing. And he knew she regularly lost things so he'd be glad when he'd secured the damn things and they were on the train.

His mind drifted unexpectedly. Kelsie used to lose things all the time too.

He snapped back to the present and the frown he sent his grandmother must have been more ferocious than he thought because she burst out laughing.

'And will you cut off my head if I don't?'

'What?'

'Give you the tickets. You have serious control issues.' She shot him a penetrating glance. 'Thinking of other things, were you?'

Lord, he'd forgotten how easily she read him. 'No.' He took the tickets she offered. 'And thank you,' he added, his voice dry. This journey could prove very tiresome if Winsome decided to tease him for most of it.

He moved into line behind a young woman buried

in what looked like a 1940s ankle-length trench coat
two sizes too large for her, and the fur of the collar was
pulled up around her ears. When she darted a look at
him all he could see was the bridge of her nose under
her dark glasses and the thick black hair scraped back
off her high forehead.

'*Buon giorno,*' he said.

'*Buon giorno,*' she whispered back, and turned away.

Maybe she was a very young secret agent? This trip
had the makings of a farce already, he thought sardonically, and glanced ahead to another older lady around
his grandmother's age, though not as well looking come
to think of it, accompanied by a younger woman.

He narrowed his eyes thoughtfully. That could be
an answer. Distract Gran with a kindred spirit. Maybe
arrange to have them sit together at dinner. He glanced
at the girl. She had a nice smile so even if Gran tried to
pair him off with someone else, it wouldn't be too bad.
Anywhere away from Kelsie Summers.

Truth be told, he didn't understand why he was
dwelling on such a chance encounter with a woman
he'd once fancied in his youth. Well, maybe a little more
than that but it wasn't like he'd carried her with him for
all these years—or been celibate. Far from it.

Neither had he found anyone else he could think of
joining his life with, a sardonic voice inside suggested,
and he impatiently brushed that thought away. A full-
time relationship was the last thing he required. He seriously didn't have time.

The line moved forward and he wondered idly where
the luggage for the woman in front was.

Which made him shoot a glance back at where Kelsie's Suitcase-asaurus Rex was, and decided it was the biggest damn thing he'd ever seen and even she'd have trouble losing that. He wondered if she knew she couldn't have it in the cabin with her and then shrugged.

And why was that his problem? What was wrong with his brain today? Thankfully the line moved forward and he directed his thoughts to move on too.

His eyes drifted back when the line stopped again. Her suitcase was still there. Might have been a stretch to think that someone would steal it anyway but...

She was back. Sitting next to his grandmother, and they looked like they were having a lovely conversation. He groaned and tried not to crush the tickets in his clenched hand. Kelsie had always been a great listener. He turned back to the line.

Insidiously, while he stared at the back of the head of the woman in front, his mind drifted to all those plans they'd had when he'd been young and stupid. Plans he'd built in his head during those impressionable teenage years that you never seemed to forget. No matter how hard you tried. The only one he had ever shared them with had been Kelsie because she'd been so much a part of his life then.

The first plan had always been—marry Kelsie. Keep her safe.

Then—become a doctor.

The third—take her to Venice on the Orient Express when they could afford it, because it was the one thing she really did have a fantasy about.

God, he'd been so stupid. He shook his head and returned to the present as the line moved forward again.

But there had been other plans and he guessed he'd at least achieved them.

He was a research-based obstetrician. Dealing with infertility. Well respected. His gran would say world renowned but he would have said he was more recognised for being happy to share what he'd learnt. He'd been very busy during the last fifteen years so it was no wonder he hadn't married.

Gran had informed him she despaired he'd find a wife before she died. No doubt she was pretty keen to see it happen but as far as he was concerned there were a lot of research projects he'd be happy to leave the family fortune to.

In fact, he had a horrible feeling this whole trip had some romantic connotation he was missing and it wasn't really about diverting Gran's mind from her recent loss. Something along the lines of if he wouldn't marry for good sense then he'd better marry for love.

Couldn't see it happening on a damn train but she'd muttered about some bloke she'd fallen for in her distant past whom she'd met on this train, and he just hoped the old man hadn't turned in his grave when she'd dropped that little bombshell.

His grandfather had been the father he'd lost the same year he'd lost Kelsie and he'd always thought his grandparents perfectly matched at least. Funny how things in life weren't always as you expected.

Like meeting Kelsie again after all these years.

CHAPTER TWO

KELSIE GLANCED AT her watch. Ten thirty-five and the train left at ten fifty-seven. She should find her carriage but seriously she wasn't ready to sit down just yet.

Winsome and her grandson had boarded, and Kelsie carried her tiny overnight satchel—thank goodness for outrageously expensive wrinkle-free clothes—and she tried to slow her agitated feet to an inconspicuous amble.

She'd been almost the last to get her ticket, mainly because she'd wanted to stay well clear of Connor, and had walked up and down the platform ostensibly admiring the ornate carriages but really walking off her agitation at seeing him again.

Connor Black. She'd loved him like a brother since fifth grade when he'd moved from being annoying to mysteriously compelling. Not that all boys had been mysterious—just Connor.

For an only child, having Connor as her friend had seemed an impossible dream, until he'd come across her being bullied by a mean-streaked older boy who'd found the purse she'd lost one afternoon, late in the spring. She could almost smell the scent of falling orange blossoms, and blood, in the orchard where it had happened.

The ensuing bout of fisticuffs had left Connor with bruised knuckles and the other boy with a black eye and split lip, for which Connor had received a caning from the school principal the next day. The thought still made her cringe because it had been her fault.

But Connor had shrugged it off as no account and her hero-worship had been sealed.

She glanced into a window of the train and her reflection smiled ruefully back at her. He'd looked so heroic, his shirt torn, his eyes narrowed as he'd warned the other boy, his gentle grasp of her hand as he'd led her away.

For the rest of that year he'd taken to walking her home, the absolute best part of her day, and she'd never felt unprotected again, even when Connor had gone off to boarding school, because the letters between them had kept them close. Because home hadn't been such a grand place, with her mother gone and her dad not much use at conversation unless it had been to give an order.

Her dad had expected her to follow the rules, and had been worse since Mum had finally rebelled and left. Although thankfully the fighting had stopped, her dad was so distant Kelsie had felt rudderless in the world until Connor. She'd wash up, do the housework and her homework, and take herself off to bed at dark, and dream of escaping to the city with Connor.

Except for Connor's correspondence, hers had been a lonely existence, lightened when holidays had come around and Connor would find her and the two would slip away to dream together.

Connor had always been full of dreams. His real mother had drowned in a tragic accident when he'd been twelve and he was always going to be a doctor, always going to save the world. And Kelsie had believed him.

When Connor went to university they would marry. Elope, Connor said, because everyone would say they were too young.

But she was content to wait until Connor said it was time and she began to have dreams of her own. To be a nurse. To be free of her father's dictatorship. Be with Connor and gladly follow him to the ends of the earth. He'd arrange everything because that's what he liked to do, and it was easier to say yes.

Finally the day arrived. Her dad forbade her to leave, Connor had forbidden her to be late, and the similarities suddenly dawned on her. Had she been using her romance to escape her father's control, only to fall into the same trap?

It was an uncomfortable thought that wouldn't go away now that it had surfaced. It was all so confusing when Connor had been so good to her.

He'd secured rooms for them near his new university, the registry office was booked, and he'd bought her a short white dress for her to wear on the train when she travelled to meet him. He'd admonished her not to daydream and miss the train. Not to lose the ticket. As if by mentioning it he could influence the vagrancies of fate.

She thought about that. And then the doubts crept in just as the hands of the little watch Connor had bought her crept closer to the time they would meet.

She loved Connor. Could see the goodness in him. How much he cared about her. But was she ready to tie herself to another man who would run her life for her so completely? Was she always going to make Connor sigh when she needed rescuing?

Was that what she wanted?

If she was having these thoughts, was it fair to rush into this and maybe one day do what her mother had done and abandon ship?

Of course she didn't want that but she knew if she tried to explain some of these thoughts to Connor, he'd brush them away as nerves.

But the seeds of doubt grew into full-grown wisdom trees on the train as she twisted the hem of the white dress between her fingers and watched the stations flash by.

Until, finally arriving, Kelsie hung back.

She loved him. The man was a serious hero. Too much of one to spoil his chance of the career he was destined for by dragging him back by her doubts. Or expect him to marry her just because he'd proposed in an impulsive moment. So she sent a note saying she was safe but she wasn't coming.

They were both too young and she wasn't able to contemplate being a burden on him. Plus there was the matter of her threatened independence. He deserved so much more but she hadn't been brave enough to tell him.

She had already seen herself frustrate him when she lost things, seen his doubts after he'd impulsively proposed, knew how much easier it would be for him to realise his dreams of becoming a doctor unencumbered by a young, unskilled bride.

The next day, after a lonely night in a sleazy motel she ran to her only other relative, her mother's much older unmarried sister, a midwife in Sydney, and that's when her life really began to change.

She'd come a long way since then. A long way.

All the way to Venice.

Kelsie blinked at the reflection in the window—the face staring back at her wasn't hers. A woman, eyebrows raised in disapproval at her invasion of privacy, stared back haughtily and Kelsie blinked. Wake up.

Her cheeks heated as she walked away. She'd been staring into the past—not the window. If she didn't watch out she'd spoil her once-in-a-lifetime trip worrying about a man who had every right to hate her.

Because maybe she should have waited to find out if Connor had agreed with her reasons. Talked about it with him. But by then it had been too late, and she'd lost touch and the confidence that he would forgive her.

And her career had taken off until the serene, confident maternity unit manager she'd become barely resembled the young girl who'd run away instead of getting married. Except for the occasional misplaced item when she was tired.

Kelsie strode purposefully up to the immaculately presented, blue-suited guard, his quaint round porter's hat stiff with its gold-trimmed peak, the whole confection jammed importantly on his head. She presented her ticket as he held out his white-gloved hand.

'Welcome to the Orient Express, madam.' He bowed, took her satchel, assisted her up the steps like precious cargo, and once she was safely aboard gestured for her to follow him up the narrow wood-panelled corridor.

Finally aboard the Orient Express, she could feel a smile plastered on her face.

'Come this way, please.'

The air inside swirled pleasantly cool around her still-hot cheeks and hinted of different perfumes and metal polish and cedar oil and old wood. Kelsie couldn't help glancing into the cabins as she followed him, interested in her fellow passengers, she assured herself, not nervously checking for Connor, and most of the passengers looked up and smiled back.

The cabin before hers held a young woman who seemed huddled in her coat, but the door was pulled shut as soon as she passed.

Kelsie winced. She was going to have a good time if it killed her or she had to kill somebody else—namely Connor Black for making her doubt herself.

The conductor stopped at her cabin and gestured grandly. 'Your seat, madam.'

Kelsie obediently sat. Not quite sure what she was supposed to do as the conductor gently hung her satchel on a big brass hook.

He stepped back, facing her, and smiled, his teeth even and white, his blond hair crew cut around his ears. 'Allow me to introduce myself.' He bowed again. 'I am Wolfgang. Your steward.'

Volfgang, she repeated to herself with an inner smile.

His English was precise and she guessed that, unlike herself, he was probably fluent in several languages. 'I vill be caring for your needs, and those others also in this car, on our way to Calais. There you vill change for the Tunnel crossing.' His precise English and accent matched his name and he suited the surroundings so appropriately, she had to smile, outwardly this time.

'Thank you, Wolfgang.' Kelsie perched on the long tapestry seat. The hanging neck pillows suspended by tapestry cords divided the seat into two. She realised she'd been lucky enough to face the direction they'd travel, thank goodness, and maybe she was even the single occupant for the next thirty-six hours. Hmm. She wasn't sure if that was a good thing or a bad one.

No. It was a good thing. She would imagine Agatha Christie with her and breathed in as she replaced the smile on her face.

Everything was perfect.

The little cabin was perfect, even prettier from the inside than it had looked when she had peered through the windows, and she noted there was only one crystal champagne flute on the pristine embossed Orient Express coaster on her tiny table so she probably did have the cabin to herself.

She sat in solitary splendour, surrounded by the dif-ferent-coloured woods of the parquetry wall panelling as they glowed with light, and she noted more brass hooks holding the deep blue silk bathrobes and velour slippers, one of which she could don should she wish to slip into something more comfortable. How deca-dent. Though perhaps not, especially at eleven in the morning.

'Observe there is a sink for washing your face and hands if desired.' Wolfgang pressed a lever and the tiny bench opposite transformed into a basin and taps. 'There is a water closet at both ends of the car.' He stared at a point at the top of the window to avoid meeting her eyes. 'It is preferred that passengers refrain from use while the train is at a station.'

Good grief. Now, that's a salubrious thought. She chewed her lip to hold in a laugh as she nodded. 'Of course,' she murmured.

He inclined his head. 'Then excuse me. When our journey begins I will return with champagne and also to record your preference for the first or second dinner sitting.'

Kelsie was tempted to ask which sitting the Blacks were on so she could choose the other but contented herself with, 'Thank you.'

She sat for a minute longer, trying to decide what to do when he left.

'Acqua Panna.' Kelsie sounded the words out on the complimentary water bottles on the bench of the washbasin hidey-hole. 'Acqua has to be water.' She picked one up, cracked the seal and took a sip as she surveyed the amenities.

Facecloths, a hand towel, a beautifully boxed cake of soap she might just keep to remind her of the journey, toothbrush and paste, an art deco folder holding postcards and embossed VSOE paper and envelopes.

Now she'd pretty well covered the contents of the cabin.

She put the bottle back and stared at the angled wooden divide opposite. They were really quite snug, these compartments, standing room only before the wall of the adjoining cabin. Someone coughed next door and she heard it quite plainly but couldn't distinguish the voices.

At least she didn't have an infectious companion

locked in with her. She grinned to herself just as the train whistle shrieked a warning of departure.

Kelsie stood and reached hastily for the table to steady herself as the carriage jerked, and peered out the window. They were easing out of the station. Her grin was back and the excitement of finally fulfilling her dream made her want to laugh.

When she poked her head out of her cabin door other occupants had crammed into the corridor and were watching through the windows opposite as the world shifted, and she could imagine the wheels on the tracks below them begin to turn and pick up speed. They slipped past two bushy islands on their little spit of railway tracks on the way to the mainland of Italy.

With a sense of urgency to take just one last look at Venice, she squeezed past an older couple in the tiny corridor and walked to the far end of the carriage, where she was able to pull down the sash window on the door she'd entered the train by.

When she leaned out the cold wind blasted her face and she could see Santa Lucia station disappearing into the distance.

She looked the other way and a dark-haired man had his head out the window half a dozen carriages up. A very familiar face turned her way and Connor Black surveyed her coolly.

Only one thing to do. Kelsie waved.

CHAPTER THREE

CONNOR PULLED HIS head in and ran his hand through his hair. He'd stuck his head out to blow thoughts of Kelsie Summers away. Fine chance of that now!

At least she wasn't in their car—she was in the last one—and he hadn't wanted to know that. He just hoped they'd chosen the right lunch sitting to avoid her.

Funny how much importance avoiding Kelsie had assumed. He hadn't spent that much brain activity on a woman for years and far too much on her today.

When he returned to their connected double cabins the steward was there.

He waved away the offered champagne. 'No, thank you.'

His grandmother gasped and leant forward to take the glass.

'For goodness' sake, Connor. If you won't drink it, I will.' She waved at the man and the obliging fellow bowed and put the second glass next to the other one.

Great, Connor thought. Now Gran was going to get tipsy and she'd be uncontrollable. This trip was assuming nightmare proportions. 'I'll drink it.'

'Good.' His grandmother sat back smugly and he realised he'd been conned and she'd never intended to have two glasses. He sighed and had to smile. She winked.

'Much better. You don't lighten up enough, my boy.'

He narrowed his eyes at her but he couldn't stay cross. She was a minx. 'It's my training. Normally, I'm responsible for people's lives.'

'You've thought you were responsible for people's lives since you were a child. Makes you bossy.' His grandmother shrugged that away. 'You've been too responsible for too long. You're becoming downright boring.'

Connor froze in the act of sipping and frowned at her. Did she mean that? Nobody else had complained—but, then, who else was there to complain?

There was a distance between him and most people that he'd acquired early, since the loss of his mother and advent of his stepmother, to be precise, and had never lost. His patients wanted him to optimise the course of their pregnancies. Fertility assistance required set boundaries of safety and precautions. Still, her comments seemed a bit harsh. 'You don't know the real me, Gran.'

'Hmph.' She snorted and he looked at her quizzically. So older ladies really did that?

She snorted again just to prove it. 'Hmph. Nobody knows you. Except maybe that girl at the end of the train.'

So this was what it was all about. And how the heck did she know where Kelsie was sitting? He'd bet Winsome had bribed the porters already, though goodness knows when as he'd only been gone a few minutes.

The she-menace had probably rung the bell as soon as he'd left.

She knew them all by name because she'd been on this train every year for the last twenty years with his grandfather. Her yearly birthday trip in February she'd missed this year because of his grandfather's death.

That had really knocked her badly and Connor, alarmed his grandmother might just fade away with grief, had hired a nurse to look after her for a few weeks to ensure she ate enough to survive. She'd begun looking much like her old self since he'd agreed to share a last journey on her favourite train.

But he was very aware this was her first Christmas without her husband and they'd decided this was as good a way as any to get over the lead up to festivities on her own.

So this was effectively a ten-month delay on her birthday train trip.

He didn't understand how she didn't get bored.

He was halfway there already, and it would be worse if it wasn't for the unexpected arrival of Kelsie Summers, and they were only a few minutes out of the station.

He sighed. So she was all over the fact that Kelsie was here! He should have known.

He enunciated carefully, as if to a child, 'You've blown it all out of proportion. She was a kid at my school and I was like the big brother she never had.'

His grandmother nodded and he could tell she wasn't listening.

She proved it. 'When you came to me you told me you'd been going to marry her.'

'Childhood nonsense. An impulse.' He shrugged. 'The girl is nothing to me now.'

She nodded, all sweetness and light, and his head went up. 'I'm pleased. I wouldn't like to see you upset.'

For some reason he didn't like the sound of that, or the way she'd said it. She glanced out the window and then back again and a horrible premonition hit him just before her next words.

'So it should be fine with you that while you were admiring the view I sent her an invitation to join us for lunch.'

Kelsie's golden envelope arrived, along with her glass of champagne, its embossed VSOE paper and the spidery writing giving a clue to its origin. She'd bet it came from Winsome.

Wolfgang hovered as she opened it and glanced at the bottom. Sure enough, the flamboyant W rolled into an exuberant salute. 'Please. Come!'

An invitation to join them for lunch at the first sitting. Fun. Not! How the heck did she answer this?

'Perhaps I should return for your answer in a few minutes?' Wolfgang wasn't slow on the uptake.

She guessed he'd been exposed to many such missives and their impact.

Kelsie smiled gratefully. 'Thanks, Wolfgang.' His head disappeared from the door and Kelsie looked down at the embossed paper again. So how did she decline politely?

She sipped her champagne, the golden fluid so surprisingly light and dry that the bubbles jumped and tickled her nose until she took it away from her mouth and looked at it. So this is what the other half drank?

Like drinking golden sunshine—no hardship at all—and she needed the courage to make a decision so she took a bigger gulp.

Or maybe she should go? Maybe that was what needed to be done. Surely inside Connor Black there was still a vestige of the hero she'd admired as a young girl and that man might understand her adolescent thinking all those years ago. He'd been her best friend and she had let him down.

The perennial questions of youth had been so important back then.

The indecision of it all. *Who does he think I am? Who do I want to be? And if I went with him would I have any choices left to me?* That had been the big one.

She still believed she'd done the right thing, but she shouldn't have been such a coward about it.

Maybe it wasn't too far-fetched that they could reconnect as friends. She hated the constraint she'd caused between them and the added bonus was she genuinely liked his grandmother.

If she sincerely apologised then surely a lot of the ill feeling would be over? It seemed he didn't mind if she came to lunch so that was a good sign.

And afterwards she could get on with enjoying her trip. Soak it all up in the way she hadn't yet started to do because of remembering her youth and Connor and her last-minute aborted wedding.

The whole trip would be over by tomorrow evening and she would have wasted it dwelling on the past.

She felt a strange sense of settlement as the decision was made. Funny how things worked out.

Wolfgang returned with the bottle of champagne and offered her a refill. She appreciated his generosity in the circumstances. 'You can tell her, yes, thank you.' She looked at her brimming glass. 'Just make sure I don't fall over on the way to lunch.'

He nodded with a smile. 'My pleasure, madam. I will return at five minutes to the hour to escort you to the correct dining car.'

'Lovely, thanks.'

Kelsie put down the glass and glanced at her watch. Eleven-thirty. And how long would lunch go on for? It couldn't be too long because the second sitting had been set for an hour and a half later and they'd have to reset the tables.

She glanced at her satchel, still unpacked. Clothes!

As the magnificent scenery of the white-capped Italian Dolomites passed, Kelsie refreshed her make-up, brushed her hair, and with a certain excitement hung up her clothes for the meal after this one.

Her aunt had always stressed it would be black tie for the evening meal on the train when she'd first mooted the idea of realising her dream, and Kelsie wanted everything to be ready when she came back after lunch.

They'd often laughed about Kelsie wearing off-the-shoulder velvet on the Orient Express, and while it wasn't velvet or off the shoulder, the black uncrushable gown was suspended by gold links of chain above her breasts and fell from beneath her bust to the floor.

Keslie studied the gown as it swayed gently on its hanger, almost Grecian in appearance, the accompanying chain belt dangling loosely at the side. The sales-woman had said it accentuated her height. She might need that if she was going to be passing Connor in the bar car.

Kelsie brushed the creases from her suit and changed the fine pale pink silk scarf for a Nile-blue one that made her smile and gave her confidence.

Her aunt had always promoted blue scarves or neck-laces. 'Excellent for the throat chakra, you know. Al-lows conversation to flow.' Well, Kelsie thought, she certainly wanted to ensure her communication skills were premium. This could be a good day for blue.

She dived back into her jewellery bag and added blue earrings and a necklace, a little over the top, she conceded, but she wanted her mouth to function well and every bit helped.

Wolfgang arrived as she'd retouched her lipstick so she squared her shoulders and picked up her purse.

'Please follow me, madam.'

'Thank you.' I'd love to, she thought sarcastically as nerves fluttered in her stomach. No. This was going to be fine.

She wobbled a bit on her heels as they walked, though she did improve the further she went. Wolf-gang didn't seem to have any problems with the slight swaying of the carriage but every now and then Kel-sie raised her hands for balance, just in case, as they rattled from side to side, and placed her feet carefully on the blue carpet.

At the end of each car the wood panelling reached new heights of intricacy, with the inlaid parquetry glow-ing with colour. Someone, maybe even Wolfgang, was handy with the cedar oil and polishing, but she had to admit the decorations were truly beautiful examples of a bygone era.

And then she saw the bar car. 'Oh, my.'

An absolute delight, the long curved bar was lit softly by lamps, and there was an ebony baby grand piano, the white ivory keys silent but, like the young passenger standing at the bar nursing his glass, waiting for the time it would be played.

Wolfgang inclined his head at the man, and Kelsie smiled as well. It wasn't hard. He was young, extremely good looking, with an admiring smile. Maybe she could spend some time in the bar before dinner.

Of necessity the carriages were all narrow, and the bar car was no exception. Tiny window seats for two slim people huddled together on one side of the narrow walkway, and on the other side a lengthwise set of couches that allowed people to sit side by side and look across the aisle and out to the magnificent scenery opposite. Tiny tables with ice buckets and wine or dishes of nuts were scattered along the length of the car.

They passed into and through the first dining car— plush velvet, crystal glasses, white-coated waiters— and into the next, which was just starting to fill with well-dressed patrons. And everywhere Christmas decorations had been discreetly tucked into unexpected corners and there was a muted background of carols playing.

Connor and Winsome were already there and Connor stood as she entered, tall, broadly jacketed, and austere as Wolfgang stopped beside their table.

Then her new friend turned and deserted her, or it felt

like desertion, and she fought the urge to follow Wolfgang as Connor indicated she should take the seat next
to him. She hadn't expected that. She gulped.

Kelsie stiffened her spine and slid across to the window opposite Winsome, trying not to shrink away as
her ex-fiancé sat back down beside her.

It was a good thing she didn't have to look at him, a
very good thing, but the warmth from his leg radiated
heat her way even though he wasn't actually touching her.

As the waiter flicked her serviette and floated it onto
her lap in a stirring of air she could smell Connor's af-
tershave, tangy and very masculine.

'Thank you,' she murmured to the man, fingering the
fine linen in her lap nervously, and then looked across
at Winsome. 'Thank you for the invitation,' she said
politely, like a little girl and then inclined her head towards the fourth setting. 'Is someone else joining us?'

The two exchanged a look but Winsome answered.
'We're not sure. Apparently the other single passenger
is feeling unwell and may not join us for lunch.'

'Oh. That's a shame.' Truly a shame. A bit of diver-
sion to leaven the stolid silence at the table wouldn't
have gone astray.

'And who is your travelling companion in your
cabin?' Winsome asked. 'I always wondered what happened if you ended with someone terrible.'

She had to laugh at that. 'I'm on my own. It's lovely
to stretch out.'

'Oh. How fortunate. But if you get lonely just come
and find us.'

Kelsie smiled and murmured her thanks, but along

with Connor she didn't comment on his grandmother's invitation.

'Would madam like a drink?'

How many hospitality staff were there? She hadn't seen the waiter arrive and she declined after a glance at the embossed wine list and thought of the glasses of bubbles she'd already downed. 'Water, please.'

'Sir?'

Connor raised his dark brows. 'Perhaps a glass of wine with lunch?' He glanced at his grandmother. 'We are celebrating your deferred birthday after all. Champagne?'

'Absolutely. Thank you.' Winsome obviously enjoyed the good life. 'Surely you'll share a glass with us, Kelsie.' Her eyes twinkled. 'It's a very belated birthday and I hate waste.'

Kelsie inclined her head to the waiter. 'One glass, then. Thank you.' What the heck. She might just need it because the vibes coming off the man beside her and even Winsome seemed strained.

It was beginning to look like Connor hadn't been too pleased after all with the invitation his grandmother had issued. She had the sudden horrible thought that maybe he hadn't even known she was coming until she'd arrived.

A different waiter appeared and stood poised with pen over notepad as he took Winsome's order and then turned to her. 'Your preference for the meal, madam?'

Kelsie looked back at the menu in her hand. 'The broiled lobster and potato and chive whirls, thank you. And the Christmas pudding.' He nodded and lifted a brow at Connor. 'Sir?'

Kelsie glanced to her left out the window and counted to ten, told herself to relax, breathe, as Connor gave his order, and almost envied the freedom of the tumbling stream that ran along beside the railway line. It looked freezing outside and every now and then they passed another house with a decorated Christmas tree in their window. The cold outside would almost be preferable to the stifling atmosphere inside.

Connor had ordered, the silence lengthened, and his leg seemed to be sending off waves of heat from beside hers, until finally she turned to his grandmother with a forced smile. 'The countryside is lovely.'

Connor was at a loss. Damn his grandmother's meddling. He felt unexpectedly blown away by the pulsing awareness he could feel just sitting next to Kelsie and that awareness was consuming him.

But as he watched her struggle for conversation, despite his own turmoil he could feel himself soften as she tried to carry the conversation by herself. She'd always been more of an enthusiastic listener. He'd probably bored her silly over the years. He should lighten up and help her out, if only for Gran.

'So tell us about Venice.'

He said it at the same time as she turned to him and blurted out, 'I'm so sorry I hurt you, Connor.'

Good grief. He hadn't expected her to go straight for the jugular. He felt his face heat, something it hadn't done for years, and he didn't like it. Not one bit. He resisted the urge to turn his head and see if anyone else had heard.

All the frustration and anger he'd damped down at the station an hour ago rose again. The last place he needed it was right here in front of everyone, and now she'd apologised he'd have to be all amenable and say that it was fine.

Well, it wasn't! She'd gutted him. But he didn't want to say that either, so he wasn't going there, and hopefully, with a hint, she would just drop it.

'Perhaps we could leave that for a less public place.'

He heard the sting in the words as soon as they were out, and regretted it. The sudden blankness of her expression almost hid her shock—but he knew it was there. A part of him even mourned the Kelsie who would have shown every emotion, but this new woman was made of sterner stuff, it seemed, and for the first time he wondered if she would give as good as she got if he really let go.

But she said, 'Of course,' and he watched her long fingers play with her scarf, his senses ignoring his cold logic of disliking her, and marvelled that the material was the exact colour of her eyes.

Then she smiled with apparently unruffled composure at his grandmother. 'Venice was gorgeous with the decorations and fairy lights, wasn't it? Where did you stay?'

They carried on the conversation without him.

CHAPTER FOUR

CONNOR WISHED NOW he had sat opposite Kelsie so he could see her face because while her profile, he had to admit, was achingly familiar, he wanted expressions and he wasn't getting any.

Not that he deserved what he wanted after such a harsh come-back to her apology. Not at all like him to speak before he thought and be unkind. He couldn't remember that last time he'd let his mouth get away from him. Consideration was in his life blood.

He was known for his unflustered take on the most emotive issues and that was why he did so well with infertility issues. Someone had to offer a clear mind. And keep it that way.

His grandmother was expounding on the virtues of the Hotel Cipriani, across the Grand Canal from the Doge's Palace, and he listened with half an ear as his libido poked him and suggested that even if he didn't want to talk about it maybe it would be a good idea to work out just why Ms Summers had left him high and dry all those years ago.

It wasn't like the thought hadn't crossed his mind once or twice since he'd last seen her.

The one time he'd tracked her down, after a mutual

acquaintance had mentioned her on one of his visits back to Australia, he'd phoned and spoken to a fellow named Steve, her fiancé apparently, and that had been that.

He glanced at her bare fingers and wondered dryly who'd run away this time? Him...or her again?

Maybe she was one of those serial bride-to-bes who made a habit of leaving at the last moment.

He remembered a movie his grandmother had made him watch and steeled himself towards Kelsie again. He wasn't sure whether it was because of the past or in response to the definite attraction he could feel pounding between them, but he was finding it hard to concentrate on anything else except the woman sitting so close to him.

He didn't like that either.

'So you spent the whole time on your own?' The voice was his but the tone belonged to a different person. Not what he'd intended and he saw his grandmother lift her brows in reproof.

Kelsie coped admirably. 'I joined tour groups and made friends at the hotel.' She raised her own finely arched brows at him. 'I'm a good mixer.'

And let him think what he likes about that, Kelsie fumed, with some acerbity. Connor Black had obviously turned into a self-important boor.

She'd learnt it was always good to keep people guessing what went on in her head, especially men, but she couldn't help feeling disappointed that her unlikely dream of being friends with Connor had slipped out the carriage window and was lost somewhere in the snow on top of the Dolomites.

Winsome looked crushed by her grandson's attitude. And it was her pseudo-birthday.

One of them had to make an effort to give the birthday girl a good time. 'Your grandmother says you deal with infertility?'

'Not personally.' He said it so dryly that she had to laugh.

Well, at least he had a sense of humour and despite the hard going at the table she was genuinely interested in his work. Winsome looked slightly relieved that Kelsie had started a conversational ball rolling that Connor might want to play with.

Funny, when what she really wanted to do was eat her lunch—or not—and get back to her cabin, but that wasn't going to happen for at least an hour. The time would pass more quickly if they chatted and she could do chat. A skill she'd learnt through her work.

She felt Connor ease his chair to the side, turning to face her a little more, and she kept her expression interested while she fiddled with her scarf below the level of the tabletop. The silk had better do its verbal soothing with her part of the conversation because she could feel words drying in her throat at the thought of carrying the whole conversation.

But it seemed Connor had finally decided to help out. 'I'm involved in research. Occasionally I work for short periods in participating hospitals and I have a few private patients.'

His voice had softened and she saw him glance at his grandmother in apology. Maybe he wasn't as bad as she'd feared. 'Did you become a nurse? I seem to remember you fancied that.'

A wee fancy for the little woman? Patronising pig. 'Hmm. Yes. And later a midwife—which is the area I work in now. So we do have a little in common.'

Thank goodness. She could talk about her work. Underwater, if needed, she loved it so much.

'I run a programme that caseloads pregnant women from their homes. Each midwife takes thirty women through the year, sees them through their pregnancies and into labour and then visits them at home for six weeks after their baby is born.'

She saw an odd expression pass across his face. 'Do they deliver in the hospitals?'

'Most *give birth* there.' She made the distinction with a little emphasis and Connor grimaced wryly at her terminology. 'A majority of the time they do, but if they want a home birth, I support them in that too.'

His eyes narrowed on hers and she could feel the current as if from another conversation simultaneously running on another level. 'Is that challenging?'

'I find it rewarding.'

'You find the challenge rewarding?'

Did he expect her to back down? 'That too.' She smiled coolly and this time he smiled back at her. Right into her eyes, and she felt herself falter.

Damn if he didn't still have it. Her stomach kicked and she looked away as the sensations swirled through her bloodstream like the stuff in her glass.

His grandmother was watching them with a speculative gleam in her eyes. No distress there. Well, at least one of them was happy with the way the meal was progressing.

She focused on the question, not on the grey eyes

that were assessing her response. 'But mostly the privilege of seeing a woman in control, in her home environment, is the ultimate reward. Women need to make the choices and wield the power in their own labours.'

And then the train whooshed past Verona station without pausing, lunch arrived, and she was saved. Eventually her pulse rate settled.

By the time they'd eaten lobster, and Christmas pudding, and finished off the bottle of bubbles, it was all okay. Even though the conversation hadn't flowed quite as smoothly as the wine it had proved less of a chore than she'd feared.

Connor had even made her laugh once or twice more and Winsome looked quietly pleased with herself.

Well, don't be thinking I'm coming to dinner, Kelsie thought to herself, and she felt Connor shoot her a glance. Good grief. Had she said that out loud?

Judging by the spark of ironic humour in those grey eyes, she just may have. It was time to go before she said something even less discreet.

She stood up. 'If you'll excuse me, I think I'll head back to my cabin and just soak in the fabulous countryside. Thank you for the wine.'

She'd seen the price on the menu, practically the price of a small car, and was quite happy that she'd earned her keep. Connor could pay for it with her blessing.

Connor watched her go. Assured, elegant, no shy young woman, this, calling to something inside him that he flatly denied, worlds away from the Kelsie he'd known.

Lord, they'd been young. She'd been the first girl

he'd ever kissed! It had taken him all day to work up the courage.

His grandmother tapped the table and he snapped out of the past, stood up quickly, and eased around behind her to pull out her plush velvet chair.

They had to pause at frequent intervals to allow other people to pass on their way from the restaurant car.

One of those people was the elderly lady he'd seen on the station. Her head turned in surprise as Winsome took another look. She wore a red jacket over a white silk shirt. The russet tones sat quite well with her flaming hair, he thought, but still it was startling.

'Lady Geraldine? Jendi?' Connor stopped and waited for the inevitable exclamations.

'Oh, my goodness. Winsome Black. What on earth are you doing here?'

'I could ask you the same thing! What an astonishing coincidence!'

Lady Geraldine's headshake was incredulous. Her red hair shone as she shook it. 'It's a small world, isn't it?'

She waved a ring-encrusted hand at the young woman accompanying her and Connor remembered seeing her at the station too.

'Winsome's an old friend that I haven't seen for years. We worked together once on a huge fundraiser for that children's charity.'

'One Last Wish.' Winsome nodded at Charlotte. 'Such a worthy cause. They made wishes come true for terminally ill children.'

'This is my granddaughter, Charlotte,' Lady Geraldine said.

'And this is my grandson, Connor.' Connor shook hands with the young woman and they both smiled at each other in mutual indulgence of people they cared about.

'She and her...fiancé are keeping me company...' Lady Geraldine's smile was poignant. 'This trip is my last wish...'

'Oh, surely not...' Winsome smiled. 'I seem to remember you telling me that age is only an attitude.'

Lady Geraldine opened her mouth but then noticed that they were creating a human traffic jam in the narrow corridor. 'We'd better get a move on,' she said. 'But we must get together, Winsome, and have a proper chat.'

He heard his grandmother say, 'That would be lovely.' No doubt it would be excruciating but he was in for the lot.

'How about afternoon tea? We could meet in the bar at, say, four o'clock?' So he wasn't invited.

Connor bit back his smile as he heard his gran's, 'See you then.' And both elderly ladies continued on their way. No doubt he could find something to amuse himself with. Or just sit in peace.

Back in her own cabin, Kelsie curled her legs up on the seat and leaned on the window to stare out. She was exhausted and yet felt strangely alive after such a fraught lunch.

Twitchy even, when wine usually made her feel sleepy.

She needed to walk but there was nowhere to go except towards a whole row of little compartments that just might contain the Blacks, and she wasn't ready to know which cabin was theirs.

Lulled by the passing countryside, the time passed in fuzzy daydreams of long walks holding hands, stolen kisses and the protectiveness of Connor's arm around her shoulders when she'd been a heck of a lot younger than she was now. She didn't want to remember and she finally stirred herself to distract her mind.

Thankfully, afternoon tea, tiny fruit custard tarts and Earl Grey tea, plus scones and cream, arrived via Wolfgang and a silver tray. She'd be ten kilos heavier by the time she finished this trip, she thought as she poured herself a long aromatic stream of tea from the silver jug he offered. She waved to a magazine on the table.

'There's a brochure with signature items for sale. So is there a shop on the train, Wolfgang?' Window shopping. Always a sure-fire way to divert her thoughts.

He smiled. 'Of course, madam. A boutique,' he corrected gently. 'In the foremost car. The boutique manager will be happy to help you.'

'Excellent. Then as soon as I finish this I might go for a wander.'

'Certainly. In a few moments the train will change direction and the bend in the track is very famous. If you watch as we navigate the curve, at one point you will be able to capture the whole train in one photograph at the correct time.'

It seemed that was a compulsory achievement as a passenger so Kelsie nodded and patted her camera until Wolfgang nodded approvingly.

'Then in one hour we stop in Innsbruck for thirty minutes to change engines. You will be able to walk around the station for a short while as well, before you dress for dinner.'

Obviously her attire wasn't suitable for the evening meal, Kelsie thought with a spurt of amusement. She wondered if she should reassure him that she would pay the proper respect to the dress codes but no doubt he would already have seen the hanging dress.

Meanwhile, afternoon tea in the bar car was even more civilised than in the carriages, and the two older ladies settled down for a lovely gossip.

'There's nothing like a *proper* afternoon tea, is there?' Lady Geraldine sighed happily as she stirred sugar into her second cup and they both listened appreciatively to the sound of silverware tapping against real bone china. 'Did you know you can buy these lovely cups and saucers from the gift shop?'

Winsome didn't like to say she'd been on this trip so many times she knew every corner of the boutique. 'I'll have to have a look. I'm planning to go there after this.'

Winsome hoped Lady Geraldine couldn't notice her nervousness. Now that she'd shaken off Connor, after their tea she was finally going to the boutique to see Max.

But in the meantime this was lovely. Meeting an old friend in the bar carriage, with the pianist now in residence playing some soft, classical music and the occasional Christmas carol thrown in.

Geraldine said, 'Maybe a set of these would make a lovely engagement gift for my Charlotte and her Nico.'

Winsome shook her head. 'You said they'd only met yesterday? In Venice? When they both saved that man's life.'

'Yes...'

She wondered if that was a tiny niggle of doubt in Lady Geraldine's voice.

'But they'd met before,' Geraldine said. 'Years ago, at Charlotte's hospital. Fate has just thrown them back together and...' She sighed again. 'It's obviously meant to be. Like your Connor and...what was her name again?'

The conversation paused for a moment as the steward removed the plates that had contained tiny sandwiches and replaced it with a platter of warm scones, adding small silver pots of jam and clotted cream.

'Mmm...' Lady Geraldine eyed the cream. 'Proper Cornish clotted cream, by the look of that.'

'Kelsie,' Winsome said, as she followed her example and picked up one of the scones. 'Kelsie Summers. But I don't think she and Connor are about to fall into each other's arms, like your Charlotte and Nico. She jilted him, in fact, fifteen years ago and I have the feeling he hasn't forgiven her.'

'Really?' Lady Geraldine spread the jam and clotted cream onto her scone and was just about to take her first bite but the conversation became more enticing than the calorie-laden treat. 'They must have been very young. Oh, *do* tell...'

Their voices dropped to a more discreet level until Lady Geraldine turned her attention back to her scone, but her expression was thoughtful.

Their voices became generally audible again. 'We might be able to help things along,' she suggested.

'What do you mean?'

'The dinner seating is very strict, I hear.'

Winsome knew that for a fact. 'It certainly is. I've

tried to change tables at the last minute on some of my previous journeys and it almost never happens.'

'It's not the last minute yet,' Lady Geraldine said firmly. 'And if we both had a little chat to the maître d', I'm sure we could persuade him to juggle things a little.'

'In what way?'

'By making an extra table available. We've still got a lot of catching up to do, haven't we? We haven't even started talking about that terrible business with Deirdre Wilkins defrauding the charity so that she could run off to the Maldives with that "personal" trainer of hers.'

Lady Geraldine's smile revealed how much she enjoyed an occasional bit of juicy gossip. 'If we asked to be seated together, that would mean leaving both your Connor and this Kelsie and my Charlotte and the lovely Nico alone at their tables.'

Winsome had to admire her friend's ingenuity. 'Yes…if we made sure they gave them a table for two or didn't put another couple to join them at one of the bigger tables.'

'It would be so romantic, wouldn't it? Everybody dressed up and the lighting all soft and lots of delicious champagne to add to the atmosphere?'

Winsome smiled. 'Why don't we ask our nice steward to go and see if the maître d' might be able to spare us a minute or two?'

'Afternoon tea was delightful,' Winsome assured Connor. Unfortunately he was already back in her compartment when she'd gone to freshen her make-up. 'Though Geraldine did look unwell.' Her own stomach felt a little queasy too but that was probably because it was nearly time.

Nerves. She was damnably nervous and she shouldn't be. It was ridiculous because she was eighty years old. But inside she didn't feel eighty.

She felt like a young girl on a first date. With a new boyfriend.

Thumping heart—Lord, she hoped it wasn't angina—and sweaty palms. At least menopause was long gone. She smiled grimly, but in fact she had nothing concrete to go on to assume the man she'd pushed to the back of her mind still felt the same as he had twenty years ago. Even then she'd been sixty, for goodness' sake. But their eyes had met and something had passed between them.

Her heart gave another flutter and she almost giggled like a little twit. She shouldn't have had so much wine at lunch but she'd needed the courage to face him.

It had been so many years of nods and handshakes, for goodness' sake, and they'd both been married at the time. It should never have happened but that lightning bolt of ridiculous magnetism had never truly been dispelled in her mind. And every year she did still think there was a special glow just for her in his dark chocolate eyes.

Max.

Ten years her junior, so gallant, so gentlemanly, so loyal to his invalid wife, as she had been loyal and loving to Robert. It had been the only thing to do.

But his wife was gone now. And so was her darling Robert. And she didn't want to spend her last years alone.

Maybe she was mad to even consider being so forward, but she knew she'd be madder not to try. She just hoped Max felt the same.

After that first year when they'd been not all that much younger and very silly, they'd indulged in one solemn stolen embrace, one magic kiss that had accepted the vagaries of cupid shooting his arrow when neither had the freedom to fly. After a long angst-filled conversation that had acknowledged the truth in their reality, they'd never physically strayed again.

The whole thing could be her overactive, aging imagination but she didn't think so. For twenty years she'd wondered and today she'd finally find out.

She'd go now. Before she lost her nerve. He might take some persuading. 'I think I'll go and have a look at the boutique.'

To her dismay, Connor put his magazine down and stood up. 'I'll come with you, Gran. Perhaps I could buy you a gift for Christmas. It's your last trip.'

Impossible. 'No. No. You stay here. I don't need anything.'

He remained standing. 'Please allow me to do that.'

She looked at him. Swallowed the disappointment and accepted the reprieve from being brave. 'Of course. That's very sweet of you. Thank you.'

Winsome's eyes went to Max's as soon as she entered the boutique and she hoped it wasn't her imagination but suddenly it did seem as if they were alone.

Still gorgeously dark and straight-backed, Max was not as tall as Connor but a lovely height to look up to. He did look older. No doubt she did too. But he still looked wonderful. She could feel her smile, the warmth in her stomach. Such a lovely man. It shone from his eyes, and every year, when she came again, without even touching her, he made her smile. Soften. Warm.

'Mrs Black. Welcome back on the Orient Express. How lovely to see you again.' Max bowed low over her hand, like he'd done so many times over the last twenty years. 'And my sincere condolences on the loss of your husband. Mr Robert was truly a gentleman.'

'Thank you, Max.' Reluctantly she drew her hand away and glanced at Connor, who stood behind her, assessing the fine glassware, sparkling jewellery, even the bound copies of Agatha Christie's novel.

'Max, I'd like to present my grandson, Connor. He was kind enough to join me on my last trip. He's come to buy me a present.'

'For your belated birthday or for Christmas?' Max held out his hand and the men shook.

Connor looked surprised and Winsome thought ironically there was a lot more he could have been surprised about. 'She did miss her birthday.'

Max smiled at Connor. 'For women as deserving as your grandmother, birthdays are sacrosanct.' Then he looked back at Winsome. 'Your last trip?'

She met his eyes and her voice lowered. 'I'm getting too old for jaunting around.' She saw his eyes soften and felt her knees tremble.

'Nonsense. Women half your age are too old. You will never reach that state.'

Winsome smiled, felt the heat in her cheeks, and turned to her grandson, hoping it didn't show. 'You see why I come here?'

'Absolutely.' His attention wandered and she relaxed.

Saw him skim the contents of the jewellery case assess-
ingly. 'Will you make a choice?'

About what? Then she remembered. 'Connor has
promised me something from your boutique for Christmas.' Her voice sounded overbright to her own ears.
She'd already said that, for pity's sake, and she tried to
tone the squeak down as an idea formed and she touched
her grandson's arm.

'Why don't you go away and have a drink in the bar
car? I can have a proper look without you glowering at
me to hurry up, then I'll meet you there and Max can
wrap it for you to collect and pay for.' She laughed and
smiled sweetly at him and he shook his head.

'You are incorrigible. But...' He grinned at Max. 'I
don't need telling twice. Enjoy.'

Kelsie's walk up the long snake of the train was like
something out of the movies. She clattered in and out of
doorways between carriages, passed people sideways in
the corridors, bumping into walls when the track jolted
a carriage unexpectedly, and always, outside, the countryside rushed past the windows.

The scenery was dotted with soaring cliffs and
turreted castles and huge suspended motorways that
curved like ribbons on stilts around the mountains.

She passed through three carriages of compartments,
the bar car, two dining cars and another three carriages
before she reached the end, and not once did she see
a dark-haired Connor or his vivacious grandmother.

Congratulating herself on her good luck prematurely,
she froze when she heard the deep timbre of his voice

as she approached the boutique—and his grandmother's laugh.

Kelsie spun back the way she'd come, she really didn't need to gatecrash their party again, but before she could slip from the carriage Connor's voice halted her.

'Is that you, Kelsie? Don't change your mind on my account.'

The hairs on the back of her neck rose and prickled. Just the way he'd said her name made the last years flash past. She hadn't expected such a visceral response.

Kelsie turned but to her disappointment there was still a neutral mask on the face she'd once known like her own. She'd be dreaming to think anything would have changed. 'Are you sure? I thought you'd be sick of the sight of me.'

Was he that bad? Connor took note of the wariness in her eyes and the challenge of unravelling the mystery of the real Kelsie Summers beckoned irresistibly—as long as he was careful.

He closed the gap between them and the expression on her face was hard to fathom. Not warm. Not cold. More assessing. But still she struck deep into his psyche in a way he remembered from all those years ago. Intriguing to imagine he did the same to her. He couldn't tell but he would like to know very much.

'It's my turn to apologise,' he said, seeking to find a way past the barriers he could feel between them. Barriers he probably deserved after their lunchtime conversation and the awkwardness he had been responsible for.

She raised those darkly arched brows and her eyes narrowed. 'For what?' It seemed she didn't trust him.

Well, that was fine by him because he didn't trust her one inch. He doubted he ever would but he was damned if he could ignore her.

So she wasn't going to make this easy. Well, he was almost glad. He wasn't sure of his plan but he did know that for the first time since he'd stood up after lunch he wasn't tired. In fact, he could feel the air crackle with sudden tension between them and again wondered just how much chemistry was left from the long-distant past—on both sides.

She shrugged those slim shoulders and time seemed to stop. She'd always done that. He'd have recognised the movement as hers anywhere. His eyes were drawn to the gentle slope of her shoulders, centred on the swell of her breasts, followed the crease upwards to her throat, where a small pulse beat under the translucent skin, and her neck rose enticingly swan-like from the cream of her silk shirt.

He wanted to slide that blue silk scarf slowly from her shoulders so he could watch it caress her neck.

'Hello? I said, for what?' Kelsie was looking at him strangely and he blinked. As well she might. He felt like slapping his forehead to wake himself up. Talk about ditherdream and dumbo. She could still scatter his thoughts.

Question? What had the question been? Ah, yes, what he needed to apologise for. 'Not making you as welcome as I should have.'

Connor considered his options. He should have added he was sorry for cutting her off in the dining car when she'd tried to apologise for the past, but he still had a bit of a knee-jerk reaction over that one. Wasn't happy with the idea she could dismiss destroying his youthful dreams with a quick apology in a public place.

But they couldn't stay here. No potential. Though why he was looking for potential in her case was a worry.

'Will you join me for a drink in the bar? My grand-mother is choosing her birthday present...' he inclined his head, indicating the boutique '...in there, and I have permission to leave her in peace so she doesn't feel rushed.'

He watched her absorb the words, and realised that watching Kelsie was actually an interesting pastime—he'd have to beware of that—and as she nodded he let out the breath he hadn't known he'd been holding.

'If you're sure you want to,' she said, and turned around again and led the way. And Connor decided walking behind Kelsie was also a spectacularly pleasant experience.

He could smell some faint unfamiliar floral scent drifting back from her and he wasn't sure if it was perfume or something she washed her hair in. Either way, he decided it was his new favourite scent.

The Christmas fairy lights made her thick bob of auburn hair shine with flashes of brilliant red and a sudden memory of playing with long strands in the sunlight when she'd worn it past her waist as a younger woman rushed into his memory as if the train had rushed through an unexpected tunnel.

'You cut your hair.'

She paused and looked back over her shoulder. 'Ten years ago.' And once again the past shimmered between them as they both remembered.

She started off again her with neat little bottom swaying gently in front of him and unwillingly his lips curved. She'd been a funny little old-fashioned girl one minute and the next a gamine seductress, and he'd loved that about her. It had always turned him on and that was another place he'd learnt his restraint.

They'd never actually gone all the way, although plenty of times he'd been sure he'd die if he didn't. They had been saving the experience for their wedding night. Well, he'd blown that chance badly.

To be fair, maybe some of that had come from his father, who'd threatened him with castration if he got a woman pregnant out of wedlock.

And look where that restraint had got him. Someone else wouldn't have been so slow to bed her—and it was incredible how bitter, even now when it shouldn't matter a jot, that thought was.

They reached the bar car without further words but it was as if they were having a conversation he couldn't quite hear. He saw her tension in the tell-tale stiffness in her neck and rigidity in her shoulders, and wondered if it was just him she was reacting to, or if she was normally a little uptight.

Or if, like him, she felt as though they were walking towards danger—becoming more delicious by the second, perhaps—but definitely danger.

Kelsie wasn't so sure this was entirely smart. It seemed to take for ever to get there and the whole time she could feel his eyes on her back. She was thinking about the dilemma of seating when they got to the bar and how to keep her distance until she'd figured out her body's responses.

The worst thing would be to knock knees on the op-posing window seats where they faced each other—no-where to hide there—and second worst would be the risk of brushing up against the full length of him if they sat together on the side lounges. She tried to remember if the fellow standing earlier had had a bar stool beside him at the bar. Yes, she thought he had. She'd head for that and see what happened.

CHAPTER FIVE

'HOW ABOUT HERE?' Connor's voice stopped her head-long dash for the bar stools. So close.

She closed her eyes then opened them before she turned with a bright smile pinned on her face. 'Sure.'

Window seat! Bummer. 'You sure your legs will fit under that table?'

'I'll manage.' He cocked an eyebrow at her. 'I'd like to see your face.'

Oh, goody. She'd been afraid of that. She slid in past the tiny table and rested her elbow on the window ledge while she jammed her knees together and pointed them at the wall.

He slid in and propped his arm on the window ledge as well. She wondered what they looked like to an observer. Probably a pair of wary dogs sniffing around each other, though a quick glance at his face showed him quite relaxed. Amused even, and she wasn't sure she liked the idea that he could be amused at her expense.

The waiter arrived promptly and Connor inclined his head towards her in mute query.

What did she want? Something that took time to drink and that she could play with when she needed to look away. 'I'll have a long gin and tonic, please. With lime.'

'Certainly, madam.' The waiter wrote her order down and she wondered why when there were so few people in the car. 'And the gentleman?'

Connor ordered a Mexican beer and slid his credit card into the man's hand before he sat back. Darn. She would have paid for her own drink this time.

'It looks cold outside,' she said finally, and glanced up at him.

This was the first time she'd really examined Connor's face up close, dared herself to really look, and the tiny signs of maturity were there if she let herself see. His bones were clearly defined still, his jaw solid, with an even more determined tilt than she remembered, but there were a few tiny lines around his gorgeous grey eyes as if from long periods of intense concentration.

His sensual lips curved as he waited and for a moment she was that star-struck young sixteen-year-old gazing in admiration at this young god who had incredibly chosen her.

For those few brief seconds he seemed to pull at the core of her until she blinked and returned to the real world. The world where she needed to get it over with and apologise and get out of here with her dignity intact—but she had to wait for the drinks.

The waiter returned and Connor raised his glass to her with a glint in his eyes. 'What shall we toast?'

She drew a breath as the man walked away. 'To apologies. I'd like to apologise for what happened fifteen years ago.'

He shrugged. Took a sip and put his glass down. 'Feel free.'

Kelsie ignored that. 'I am sorry I was a coward, Connor. But I had second thoughts about getting married to you.'

He laughed with a tiny bitter twist of his lips. 'Obviously.'

He wasn't being helpful and she could feel her temper slip a little. This wasn't easy but it had been a long time ago and he didn't need to be sarcastic.

'It didn't help that you were so sure about it that I knew if I expressed any doubts you'd just sweep them away.'

He nodded judiciously. 'Ah. So it's my fault.'

She frowned. 'No. I said I'd come and I didn't. That was my fault and I apologise for hurting you. I was a coward for not telling you my reasons on the day but I was very young. I really should have told you why.'

He leaned back in his chair and studied her face and she refused to look away. Let him look his fill. She was no shrinking violet now.

'So why did you leave me standing on the steps of the registry office fifteen years ago?'

This was the hard part. But he deserved the truth. 'We were too young. And I didn't think I was the best thing for you at that time.'

He shrugged. 'Perhaps. I obviously had no say in the matter. I can certainly see now that maybe you were too young.'

The comment held a tinge of mockery that raised her temper another notch. 'But not too young to see I was going from one controlling relationship straight into another.'

Connor felt the words go right through him. Like someone had just knifed his hand to the table and he couldn't move. 'That's not true. I was all about making sure you were safe. I wanted to look after you. Be there for you.'

She shook her head and her hair slid like a cap from side to side. 'I wasn't strong enough for you then, Connor. You organised everything. You organised me. Dressed me. You railroaded me when I wasn't sure we were doing the right thing. I was in the train coming to you before I realised it was a little too close to home. Too like the way my father had treated my mother before she left. The way he treated me. As if I didn't have a brain of my own. Wasn't responsible for anything. I didn't want us to end up like that.'

It was her turn to shrug. 'So I got cold feet.' And the air between them was getting colder too. There was no curve to his lips now. No smile in his eyes. She'd hurt him again and she hadn't intended that.

Connor had a sudden memory of his grandmother telling him he was too carefully organised. Bossy, even. It wasn't true. If you didn't make sure things were done a certain way then bad things happened. He'd learnt that early on in life. In the worst possible way.

'I think you had it wrong. I only wanted what was best for you,' he said quietly.

She spread her hands. 'You're entitled to think that. But I still think I was right. I should have confronted you on the day, I know that. Only I was too scared you'd sweep my fears away. But I am sorry I hurt you.'

You don't look sorry enough, Connor thought bitterly. 'Well, thanks for that.'

She stood up. At least it saved him doing it. Clearly, this conversation was only going to deteriorate from here.

'My pleasure,' she said, and internally he winced. Their little talk hadn't turned out quite how he'd hoped.

She looked down at her barely touched glass. 'Thanks for the drink. Enjoy the rest of the trip with your gran.'

She walked away, her dignity intact, and he wondered just how close she'd been to losing her temper. He had a sudden thought that she might have been very close to an explosion. He'd have liked to have seen that and maybe then they would have been on an even footing.

But Connor felt incredibly hard done by and actually quite wild on his own part. So it had been *his* fault for not listening when she'd had second thoughts about getting married? Well, if he'd realised just how cold her feet had been he would have listened. He wasn't a mind reader.

He'd been a romantic! He'd arranged flowers and chocolates for after the wedding back at their flat. A bottle of champagne he'd been unable to afford in the fridge because he'd thought she might need a glass before they made love for the first time. He'd wanted everything to be perfect for her.

And she'd said he was too organised! But someone had to be. Didn't they?

He downed his beer and picked up her gin and tonic. It tasted disgusting but he drank it anyway. Well, she was no immature girl now. She was fair game. So game on!

* * *

Half an hour later, as they entered Austria, Connor saw Kelsie sweep off the train in Innesbruck. Her long scarf trailed behind her as she strode up the platform and he decided a breath of fresh air would be just the thing.

He'd spent the last thirty minutes going over their conversation. Too bossy, eh? He was going to be so damn deferential he'd drive her crazy. He didn't know why it was so important to let Kelsie know she'd missed out on the catch of a lifetime but there was definite satisfaction in the thought, and the next twenty hours was a large amount of time to kill with nothing better to do. Then they would really be over.

A sardonic voice inside enquired if he was sure of that...

When he climbed down the steps she was sweeping up and down the platform like a ghost was after her and he had an idea his younger self may have been that illusion she was escaping from.

Well, he needed to banish that phantom too if he was going to win this little battle. He wasn't quite sure when it had become a war but he was in no doubt that he was planning one.

He'd walked the other way so that she was almost ready to board again before he approached her, and he saw her eyes widen as he came near.

'Kelsie. Just one minute.' And he smiled. Very friendly. Slightly rueful. 'Can I apologise again?'

She raised those truly quite delightful eyebrows and he admired the view as he waited for her to speak. 'For what?'

They both watched Wolfgang polish the fingermarks

off the handrail with his white gloves as he stood beside the steps.

He lowered his voice. 'My lack of manners. I'm sorry. I was less than gracious earlier and of course I accept your apology for not marrying me.' He smiled again.

It seemed she wasn't ready to board now, but maybe the impact would be greater if he chose to leave, so he inclined his head and climbed the steps, leaving her alone again. He could feel her eyes on him as he disappeared inside and he chewed his lip to stop laughing out loud.

He felt like that blasted nineteen-year-old again as he went in search of his gran.

The bar car was crowded when Kelsie moved through the doorway to join the pre-dinner throng and her long black gown clung lovingly to her breasts and thighs. At least it wasn't falling off.

She'd missed the first ten minutes of pre-dinner drinks when one of the gold-linked straps holding up the bodice had snapped and she'd needed an urgent repair.

One-handed, she'd called for Wolfgang, who'd swooped to the rescue with a tiny pair of pliers on request.

She'd decided that taking the extra time to check and squeeze each link could be an investment in preventing her future embarrassment. Even with the repairs the bodice of the gown dived a little lower into her cleavage than she remembered but not as low as it would if the strap broke. The last thing she needed was Connor coming to her rescue from a wardrobe malfunction. He'd done that in the past too.

The bar wasn't full, but her aunt had been right about formal dress. Wow!

The pianist was in a velvet brocade jacket that would have done justice to a very swish couch cover and his music soaked the car with waves of pleasure like the scenery outside—sometimes soaring, sometimes gentle, always melodic and accompanying the sound of the rails below.

Scattered on small tables and along the curved bar were bowls of nuts, *petits fours* and canapés, and all the while through the windows she could see white-capped mountains and white houses with Christmas lights and church spires and tumbling mountain streams.

And inside, just as grand, the men were in dinner suits with bow ties. The maître d' wore black tails and the waiters wore formal white.

The same young man was still at the bar, a little less steady, and he leered when he saw her.

'You look beautiful, madam.'

Kelsie smiled back at him carefully, and decided he was too young for her, and a bit too effusive.

'Doesn't she?'

She had no idea where Connor had come from but he was by her side as he smiled at the man. His shoulders looked very impressive in his black dinner suit and the young man suddenly seemed insignificant. 'Would you like to introduce me to your friend, Kelsie?'

What on earth was Connor doing? 'If only I could,' she said, and held out her hand to the man. 'I'm Kelsie.'

The bar fly was happy to take her fingers. 'Winston

Albert the Third.' He shook her hand and they both looked at Connor.

'Connor Black.' He glanced down the carriage as more people arrived. 'Ah. My grandmother beckons. Perhaps you'd like to join us, Kelsie? Or later?'

He didn't move off immediately, but there was no hint of pressure either way, and Kelsie couldn't help feeling a little abandoned, which might have been why she found herself taking Connor's arm as she nodded goodbye to the other man.

She had the feeling she'd been outmanoeuvred. She wasn't sure how when it had all been her choice, but the feeling persisted.

The train jolted suddenly, the whole carriage shifted and there was a small outcry, and she probably would have fallen if Connor hadn't caught her. He looked down at her and grinned as he steadied her against his chest for a moment as their bodies remembered one another. Instant, scorching heat flared between them as their eyes caught and held.

'Are you starting a new habit of saving me?' she asked with a shaky laugh, and he raised his brows.

'Do I need to?' he asked softly.

She blushed and looked away. On the tiny scrap of dance floor a young couple had turned a near accident into an impromptu waltz and their obvious absorption in each other cast a glow over the whole carriage, so people were smiling despite a few spilt drinks. There was a brief round of applause for the dancers when they separated.

Further down the carriage, Winsome, dressed in blue shot silk, had somehow managed to secure a full side-facing seat and sat with another elderly lady with flaming red hair who waved hands laden with diamonds.

Kelsie's fingers rested over Connor's arm and he drew her forward so she had no choice but to intrude on the older women. 'Lady Geraldine, this is Kelsie Summers. A friend from my school days.'

He gestured to the older lady. 'Kelsie, Lady Geraldine, who sat on a committee of a large charity with my grandmother several years ago.'

Lady Geraldine inclined her head, Kelsie smiled, and then sat when Winsome patted the sat beside her.

Why did she feel the jaws of a trap were closing around her?

'Winsome and I have arranged a table for ourselves,' Lady Geraldine said, as if continuing a conversation Kelsie had missed the start of. 'We don't want to bore you young things with our gossip.'

The implications were immediately obvious. Another man and Connor exchanged a glance, as if they were measuring each other up and considering the prospect of a foursome for dinner.

Kelsie was watching the older women as if she knew there was more coming. And there was.

'Instead, we have three tables.' Geraldine smiled. 'One for each couple.'

Charlotte, the granddaughter, looked as if she wanted to groan aloud. 'I don't think you're allowed to change arrangements like that, are you, Gran?'

Lady Geraldine merely tapped the side of her nose. 'Wait and see where the maître d' puts us all,' she murmured. And then she winked at Winsome. 'Being old doesn't entirely deprive us of our ability to charm men into doing what we want, does it, Winnie?'

'Not at all, dear. As you say, age is only an attitude.'

Winsome seemed surprised when Connor didn't demur at her seating arrangements. She wasn't the only one surprised. Kelsie hadn't thought Connor would enjoy being organised by someone other than himself.

'Absolutely. I'm sure you and Lady Geraldine have a lot of catching up to do. I'm quite fine sitting with Kelsie if that's what you've arranged. As long as Kelsie doesn't mind.'

Kelsie declined to comment but decided she needed a drink for fortitude.

Connor must have picked up on her thoughts because he disappeared and returned with a glass of champagne. He handed it to Kelsie as if it was his lot to meet her needs, and she decided something was going on here because the vibes were *so-o-o* different from those at lunch and certainly different from when they had parted that afternoon.

And now they'd have to sit together, alone, for a formal dinner.

She took another sip and wondered what the alcohol content in her blood was running at since boarding this darned train and whether it was interfering with her usual caution.

Conversation flowed remarkably easily until the gong went for dinner. The bar car had filled up, men and women flashed their jewels and fabulous clothes, stilted conversations merged into introductions as strangers tried to make conversation as they waited to be allocated their tables.

Kelsie felt the heat in her cheeks as Connor stood attentively beside her. People dodged the champagne buckets and others milled and chatted in the small space as they waited.

Finally the loudspeaker encouraged the patrons to go through to dinner, first in English and then in French, as the waiters checked off names. Kelsie stood with Connor and walked through to the next car and their table.

Connor beat the waiter to her chair and pulled it out for her, helping her to move it back in when she was seated, and she looked down at the table, suddenly feeling embarrassed. He'd always had such beautiful manners. It had been one of the lovely aspects of spending time with Connor away from home. He'd always treated her like a princess.

The table was crowded with crystal glasses—four sizes each and all engraved with the VSOE insignia—three sets of silver cutlery, fine china with the crest again and crested doilies under everything to stop any hint of slippage from the motion of the train. She marvelled at the thought of the relaying of the tables for the next sitting.

Their waiter arrived, carrying Connor's champagne bucket, and he skilfully topped their glasses despite the sudden jolts. They both smiled at his dexterity.

Connor broke the silence between them. 'So my grandmother has been at work again.' Connor settled back into his chair and smiled. 'Can you stand another meal with me or would you like me to ask to be moved?'

'Of course not.' There wasn't a lot she could do about it now and it could have been a whole lot worse. She might have had to keep the bar fly under control. Instead, she had a handsome man who had once been her lifeline. 'I'll be able to handle it for one more meal. I think breakfast is in bed tomorrow morning so I'm safe.'

'I'll look forward to it.' His mouth curved, smiling and sexy, a deadly combination that encapsulated her in their private joke, and the room seemed suddenly a little too warm again.

'Even your grandmother couldn't arrange that,' she said dryly, and he smiled again. She almost wished he wouldn't do that. It was a devastating smile and if her shoes hadn't been so tight her toes might have curled.

He glanced down at the menu and then back at her. 'So, what are you having?'

She looked down, scanning the options you could purchase before she looked at the meal that was included, and gasped. 'I think I'd rather buy a coat at Harrods than a serving of Beluga caviar.'

He glanced at the price of the optional entrée and winced. 'We could both buy a coat.' He grinned at the à la carte menu for those too fussy to have what the chef de cuisine suggested. 'Shall we have the Christmas dinner menu, then?'

She nodded vigorously. 'Indeed. I'll have the traditional roast turkey with chestnut stuffing and dessert of a classic plum duff with *crème Anglaise* and brandy butter.'

'Good choice. I'm not a turbot fan myself.'

She laughed. He was funny. It was easy. They were conversing as if all the tense conversations of the day had been swept away and she could feel the stiffness in her neck begin to subside. The feeling of relief was heady. And he was charming. She might just have to watch that.

'The fellow at the bar was right, you know.' His gaze rested on her face.

'What?'

'You look very beautiful in that dress. In fact, you've looked beautiful all day.' He wasn't looking at the dress. He was watching her face and she felt the warmth steal into her cheeks. 'You look even more beautiful than you did fifteen years ago.'

Now her cheeks burned and she didn't know where to look. The obvious place was at him. Dark dinner suit, white shirt and bow-tie. Sardonically suave yet with a twinkle in his eye. 'Thank you. You look pretty hot yourself.'

'I was hoping you'd say that.' His face became more serious. 'So why haven't you married, Kelsie?'

'Why haven't you?' she countered.

He shook his head. 'That's a cop-out and I asked you first. I had the impression you were a brave new you. Don't be shy. I'm sure it's not because you haven't found anyone who exceeded my charms.'

'Oh, you're charming, too, but way too old for me. I'm looking for a younger man now. Like our friend at the bar.'

She'd been trying to keep it light, not sure they were quite at ease enough to get down to real truth. That it would take someone pretty darned special to make her give up the independence that she'd fought so hard for.

She wasn't going to make the same mistakes her mother had made and if she never did get married and have a child at least she wouldn't walk away from them like her own mother had.

She was starting to feel more emotional than she wanted to. Here was this gorgeous man, flirting with her, and all she could remember was how she'd left him standing alone on a corner. How worried his face had been. It made her feel bad. And sad.

'So you think I wouldn't be able to keep up with you?' His hand reached across the table and he squeezed her fingers, stroked the inside of her wrist, and she shivered. There was that unmistakable frisson of awareness that assured her they still had far too much chemistry happening for her peace of mind.

His hand moved back away from her and instantly she missed the connection. 'I'm willing to bet I could.'

Her fingers tingled. It wasn't fair that he could do that with just a touch and she'd always thought the whole vibration in auras between a man and a woman had been exaggerated. 'You seem determined to put a personal spin on all my words but you can never go back.'

Her mouth was saying things her body didn't agree with but it seemed appropriate when she wanted to create a distance he was trying to close. Her imagination wasn't helping with fantasies of finding out just what would happen if she crawled into Connor Black's lap and kissed him.

He was watching her face and unfortunately there was nowhere to hide. 'Today I was thinking about our first kiss.' His voice dropped and she leaned forward to hear. 'You were soft, like a kitten.'

She bounced back into an upright position, blushing

like a schoolgirl, and it was her turn to hope nobody had heard or could see the pink in her cheeks. 'And you missed my mouth the first time.'

He smiled lazily. 'I'm better at it now.'

That made her smile and instantly the rapport was back. 'You weren't so bad even then, once I got over the shock.'

Thankfully the meal arrived and it should have been easier but her eyes strayed to his strong white teeth as he put the fork to his lips, that tilt to his wicked mouth and his strong throat.

She tried to work out what was pushing her buttons. He was unmistakably the full package when you put his undivided attention and the close proximity of their bodies together. Plus the memories of their slow awakening as they'd grown to adulthood together all those years ago.

Would things have been different if they'd made love before their wedding day? The room was getting hot again.

Connor watched the play of emotions cross her face. Every now and then he caught glimpses of the young girl from so many years ago. A vulnerability he thought she'd lost that made him want to protect her, but he stamped that down. No way. She didn't want him to, and had never wanted him to. That was why she'd left him, remember?

But that wasn't all he saw. He saw the pulse beat at her throat, the subtle lushness of a woman's body that stirred him like no other woman's had. He could still feel the silk of her skin when he'd squeezed her hand that had burnt right through his defences so that he'd had to let go. There was no doubt he was playing with fire but hopefully neither of them would get burnt.

He sat back and let the tension ease. They still had eighteen hours to go and he wasn't rushing into anything.

Selected cheeses, the plum duff with *crème Anglaise* and brandy butter, a sun-kissed dessert wine to be sipped and between them awareness swirled like the gold in the glasses as they smiled over firsts together.

First hand-holding—how nervous she'd been. First kiss—how nervous he'd been.

First fight and whose fault it was—not able to agree on that one.

Old memories. Good memories that had been overlaid by guilt and shame and a lack of communication that now they could only shake their heads at.

Both of them warmed to the shared moments that, despite the years, seemed like yesterday now they'd been allowed to escape.

He glanced away to where a tiny Christmas tree spun in a corner with fibreoptic branches lighting the heads of the people sitting nearby in subtle colours.

He tilted his head towards it. 'Do you remember?'

She glanced across and he saw the smile in her eyes as she nodded. 'It was the year before you went away to school. My father had thrown out the old tinsel tree we had and I was heartbroken we weren't having a tree. So you bought me a tiny little tree like that, with decorations and fibreoptic lights that came on when I plugged it in. I kept it in my room and it made me smile at night.'

'I was so excited when I saw it but your father hated it.' He smiled and shook his head. 'And he hated me.'

She shrugged. 'He hated everyone. It was a lovely thing to do. If it hadn't been for you Christmas would have been the same as any other day in the year.'

He thought about it. 'You made my Christmas special just by being there.'

Kelsie couldn't believe how light she felt. As if she'd found a dear friend she'd thought she'd lost. And that was what it was. Impulsively she reached across the table and took his hand. 'I'm so pleased we've had tonight.'

He brought his other hand over the top and held her hand on his. 'So am I.'

Then he lifted her hand to his lips and kissed it gently, and suddenly she didn't want to be in this car any more.

He must have seen that. 'There's not a lot of places to go but would you like to walk?'

CHAPTER SIX

AWAY FROM PEOPLE? Should she?

Not that they'd do anything they couldn't in front of witnesses. Witnesses. She shied away from the word, like a wedding that hadn't happened, thank goodness she hadn't said that out loud—but, yes. She'd like to go somewhere quieter. More private.

Connor rose and pulled out her chair, waited for her to precede him in the direction of her cabin, not his, and then followed at her shoulder so she could feel him brush against her as she made her way past tables filled with crystal and silver and satiated patrons.

People she didn't see. Past his grandmother, and the red-haired lady, and the couple who had danced, and always Connor's hand hovered below her waist in case she lost balance with the rock of the train. So she was safe from injury but moving forward towards a different sort of delicious possibility.

Her senses seemed more alert. Her skin more sensitive when he brushed against her. Her peripheral vision seemed filled with him and it was a very strange sensation amongst a sea of sensations.

Connor leaned forward and opened the door for her,

and for a crazy moment she wanted to bury her nose in his shirt and have him wrap his arms around her.

She wasn't even sure he liked her but maybe there would be time for that later.

She couldn't help the smile that curved her lips as she looked up at him and his hand tightened on her shoulder.

'Best not to look at me like that when we're in public,' he murmured with a wicked hint of warning in his voice.

Her stomach kicked and her face flamed. What were the rules for a first date with someone you'd once loved? Someone you'd thought about on and off over the last fifteen years. Someone you'd once known as well as yourself and who'd always left you deliciously alert. She'd never known him that way—though they'd had a few close shaves—but Connor had always said he'd wait until they were married.

But that had been then and this was now. Now they were both consenting adults with no ties. She was no longer a virgin—and it would be highly unlikely that a gorgeous man like Connor would be one either.

They passed through the bar car and she didn't see anyone. Just a blur of obstacles to avoid. Was she being too forward?

Would he think she'd turned into a nymphomaniac if she asked him to bed? Because that was what she was thinking, though it could be problematic in a small train with very thin partitions between the cabins.

His hand stayed in the small of her back, hot and possessive and the tension eddied and churned between them and her belly swirled with a mounting ache that had her squirming as she walked faster than she probably should have towards her cabin.

They came to a deserted corner between carriages and he leaned her against the wall and pinned her there. His face was all angles and intent and a hint of a smile in his eyes as he took his time studying her face.

'Now. About that first kiss...' This time he didn't miss and Kelsie felt her head bump back against the polished rosewood parquetry as she melted bonelessly against him. His mouth was strong and hot and demanding and she couldn't have denied him if all the passengers had trooped past them.

His hand was in her hair, absently rubbing where she'd bumped it, murmuring against her lips with a smile in his mouth, and she kissed him back with all the angst of fifteen years of regret and apology and finally pure desire, and became lost.

Then someone did come along, coughed and made a small joke, and they broke apart. Kelsie smiled down at the carpet, avoiding the face of the other passenger, and heard Connor's relaxed, 'Good evening.' How could he be so cool? She not accidentally, though unobtrusively, brushed his thigh with the back of her hand and heard his indrawn breath. Still able to smile and pretend nothing was going on, Connor?

She glanced up at him as the footsteps died away and his eyebrows hiked as he smiled down at her.

'My, my. Haven't you grown up?' He leaned in again and flattened himself into her so that she could feel the length of him pressed solidly against her. He grinned lazily. 'Has anyone seen Kelsie?'

'I'm here. And you've been practising your kissing.'

'Fortunately.' They both smiled as he stepped back, took her hand and led her into the next carriage, and then the next, until they stood outside Kelsie's door and she opened it.

Kelsie put her fingers to her lips. Inclined her head towards the cabin next door. 'Sh.'

He leant down until his lips just brushed her ear and she shivered as he whispered, 'I can do quiet.'

Kelsie decided there was something very intimate about whispering in a darkened compartment on the Orient Express.

Especially when golden chains of her dress had been lifted aside and Connor Black was spreading wonder over her bare skin as they stood pressed together in the darkness of her cabin. It was all a blur of whispers and touches but mostly it was feeling Connor's mouth against hers.

Every few minutes a bell would ring and lights from a railway crossing would flash lights across their faces, and once she opened her eyes to see him staring at her as he stroked her cheek.

Time passed. They kissed like they could never kiss enough. Whispered about their lives, their dreams, their regrets and their successes. Held each other, Kelsie even shedding a few tears, and they laughed very quietly. Reconnected.

Connor was trapped. He wanted to take Kelsie more than he wanted to breathe but he feared the exposure. The ripping open of a protective shield he needed to survive.

He couldn't do it.

Already she'd burrowed under his defences more

than he would have believed possible. Though he'd been young, he had truly loved this woman. Would have given her everything. The problem was he was whole now and he didn't trust her not to hurt him again.

He'd survived once when he'd lost her and he wasn't so sure he would survive again if she touched his soul in giving herself to him. Making love with Kelsie, the way they were sparking off each other tonight, promised to be no light undertaking.

He didn't know if he would ever really trust her again. Surely it would be a hundred times worse if they made love and she got off the train in London and walked away.

Yes. It would. He could feel his sanity return.

For a few moments there he'd been ready to burn in hell if he could bury himself in her. But he was damned if he was going to rue the day he met her again.

Connor pulled the gold straps back up her shoulders and kissed her once more.

Kelsie sat back and stared at him. 'Is something wrong?'

'Everything is perfect. Let's not spoil it.'

He saw her disappointment. Well, he had dibs on that one from a long time ago, and tonight he was right there with her. But he'd been burnt once by her. Severely, and he didn't do loss well.

And he wasn't going to do something he'd regret. Funny how it had only been that way with Kelsie. Seemed he was better at denying himself than she was, which made him feel slightly better.

But this was the new Kelsie and again she surprised him.

Connor had drawn the line. Again. Heck, she'd

thought he'd got over that, she grumbled to herself in the throes of frustration! She sat upright from where they'd ended up entangled on the seat, pushed back her hair and straightened her straps properly. For the first time in her life she'd actually been totally swept away. Scary, scary stuff.

She took a few good breaths and focused. 'Well, that's a turn-up for the books. It's usually me who stops the action. Different, but probably sensible.' She looked at him with a crooked smile. 'Thank you. I think.'

'And I think I'd better go.'

She arched her brows. 'Before I jump you again?'

He smiled. 'It is a worry.'

She wondered at the underlying truth beneath his jokey statement as she watched him leave.

CHAPTER SEVEN

FIFTEEN MINUTES LATER, ready for her solitary bed, Kelsie was feeling pleased with herself. She'd visited the end of the rocking carriage and marvelled at the flash of railway tracks below the white porcelain bowl with a sort of horrid fascination.

Wolfgang had been in and made her long seat into a snug little bed with starched white sheets and satin-bound woollen blankets. There was a delightful old-fashioned tin of sweets, of course in a blue-lined crested container, resting on her pillow, and the nightlight had been switched on.

Outside the window, snow flew in little flurries and the muted bells of the passing railway crossings added a soothing melody to the sound of the tracks clacking below.

But as she cleaned her teeth at the tiny basin, she stared at her pink cheeks in the gilt-edged mirror and wondered at the star-filled eyes of the woman who stared back.

She still reeled at the absolute mindlessness Connor could induce when he kissed her. Her cheeks glowed back at her as she thought about her lack of control. Somewhere inside her the unsatisfied woman within

grumbled and groaned at an ache that wouldn't go but
still she marvelled that after all these years Connor
was the one who could make her legs give way when
he kissed her.

It seemed she wasn't uninterested in sex after all.
Sex was pleasant, nice, occasionally great, but just kissing someone had never shaken her rafters like Connor had tonight. She grinned at the thought. Did trains
have rafters?

A small smile teased at her lips as she dried her
mouth. And to think that she'd wished she hadn't seen
him in Venice. They wouldn't have much time when
they got to London but maybe it wouldn't be a solitary
Christmas after all. She had a few hours before she flew
away. The possibility of spending a little more time with
a very grown-up Connor Black before she left would
be a bonus and she would be very interested in that.

Not that she minded being on her own for Christmas, as she usually worked and the thought of wander-
ing around the deserted streets of London on Christmas
morning had been part of the plan.

They hadn't actually spoken about what would happen when they arrived in London but they had hours
of travel to go. It was perfect that she was leaving the
next day because the tiny voice that wanted to start
planning a life with Connor didn't have a chance. That
was good. She enjoyed her independence too much to
be answerable to any man. Even Connor Black. Especially Connor Black.

For the rest of the night she was actually quite looking forward to some cheeky dreams in her rocking bed.
She switched off the light above her bed and let the dim-

ness soak into her. Despite her solitude, her cabin still seemed to hold the essence of Connor and she closed her eyes dreamily.

The crying started just as Kelsie's head sank deeper into the pillow. The darkness carried the soft weeping that came every few minutes and rose and fell like a tiny wave.

Her eyes opened again and Kelsie glanced at the luminous hands of her watch. The sound went away and she closed her eyes.

It came again. Three minutes since the last.

She knew about those tiny waves. Sat up and stared at the wall opposite.

The noise returned, intensified, and she tracked it to the wall behind her head—from the compartment that held the girl in the oversized coat.

She climbed out of bed and pulled on the blue silk robe and her soft Orient Express bedroom slippers and sighed. Though not sure of her reception when the girl had tried so hard to remain out of sight, Kelsie couldn't leave her to weep alone.

Especially when she had her suspicions as to why a woman might be crying like that.

Kelsie unlocked her compartment door and peered out into the corridor. Apart from the clatter of the wheels on the rails beneath them, the corridor was silent—until the girl began to weep again.

All of the hallway doors she could see were shut and she suspected that nobody else wanted to investigate. It had to be well after midnight but the sound floated in tendrils down the corridor.

Kelsie tapped gently on the door next to her. The crying stopped and there was a shuffling noise and then the door opened a crack.

'Are you okay?' Kelsie whispered through the crack, and the door opened a fraction more.

A shaky whisper came back, 'No. I am afraid.'

Afraid wasn't good, Kelsie thought, and hardened her resolve to intrude. 'Can I come in? I'm alone.'

No answer for a long pause and then the door opened enough to allow entry and Kelsie slipped around the door and then pulled it shut quietly behind her.

The girl climbed back into bed and curled into the foetal position as if she could keep away the pains. Kelsie couldn't really do anything except stand over against the door or sit next to her on the rumpled bed.

She was young, dressed in a thin white nightgown, and when Kelsie looked down the obviousness of the pregnant belly confirmed her suspicions.

'I'm Kelsie. Can I sit for a minute?'

The slim shoulders shrugged and the woman sniffed, but she shifted her bottom further back into the bed so there was room for two. 'I am Anna.'

'Hello, Anna.' Kelsie peered into her face. 'Are you in labour, Anna?'

Anna shook her head in the negative, rapidly, and then sighed. 'I don't know.'

'How long have the pains been coming?'

Huge dark eyes stared solemnly back as the girl pushed her thick long black ponytail off her neck. 'Since we left Venice.'

'Are they regular?' The girl blinked and didn't answer. Kelsie tried again. 'Do they come the same distance apart? Every few minutes.'

'I think so.' Her eyes screwed up and her hand flew to her belly. 'Another comes.'

The young woman began to whimper and Kelsie put her hand on her shoulder. 'It's okay. Just let it happen. Don't be scared. If you're scared then you feel more pain. Keeping calm means less pain.'

Kelsie listened to her automatic midwifery patter and mocked herself. *Or you could be scared because you're in a train in the middle of the Swiss Alps and there's snow outside. If something goes wrong, we're all in trouble.*

Instead she said, 'Just let it go. Let it wash over you like a big wave. Ride it up one side of the wave and down the other and let it go. Everything is fine. You're doing beautifully.'

She could feel the tension ebb away under her fingers as she squeezed the woman's shoulder gently and hoped to goodness this baby was a decent size because the tummy beside her didn't look that big.

'When is your baby due?'

'I don't know.'

It wasn't an answer she wanted to hear but there was nothing to do about that now. 'Have you seen a doctor at all while you've been pregnant?'

'The doctor would tell my parents.'

Who must be very well known? Or perhaps it was a small town?

Mentally Kelsie grimaced. *There are doctors out there who don't know your parents,* she thought, but tried again.

Obviously money wasn't a problem if she could hire a single compartment on the Orient Express. It had taken Kelsie three years to save up for this trip so the issue wasn't financial.

'Have you been well?'

'Until today when the pain started.'

'And do you remember when your last period was?'

'*Non.*' Anna's eyes widened again and she began to hyperventilate.

Kelsie put her hand back on the young woman's shoulder and talked her through that contraction as well. It seemed to last longer and be more powerful than the previous one, which was never a good sign on a train, Kelsie thought resignedly.

She was so young. As young as she had been when she'd left Connor. She could remember what that felt like. Terrifying. 'Does the father of your baby know you're pregnant?'

'*Non.* But I go to tell him.' Her eyes grew rounder. 'In Paris. He is meeting me.'

He might meet more than you if the contractions get much stronger, Kelsie thought, and decided it was time for reinforcements.

She shifted on the seat so the girl could see her face more clearly. 'Anna, I am a midwife. A nurse for babies. You understand?'

The girl nodded. 'I think perhaps you may have your baby in the next few hours. We have to get you to a hospital until after your baby is born.'

Vigorous shaking of the head ensued. 'No. I will be in Paris in five hours. I will wait.'

Kelsie smiled. I wish, she thought. 'Your baby may not wait.'

More head-shaking. 'Leave me. I will not get off the train!'

Kelsie could almost understand her reluctance. It was dark. Midnight or later. Goodness knew where they were and if anyone spoke a language this girl understood if she did get transferred to the nearest hospital. And how hard would it be to be transferred out again after the baby was born?

But the reality was it was a very tiny cabin. And this was a train! 'Look, I believe babies of healthy young women are generally born healthy. But if something did go wrong you have no back-up plan. No way to save your baby if he or she needed emergency help. No way to save yourself if you needed help.'

She pushed away the thought of Connor a few carriages away. Just because they had an obstetrician on board, it didn't mean they had anything else.

Anna shook her head violently and then began to breathe rapidly again as the next contraction built and Kelsie saw the wildness enter her eyes. It seemed Kelsie might just need back-up very soon.

'It's okay,' she whispered as she leaned forward and pressed the call button for Wolfgang. Perhaps he could talk some sense into their friend.

This contraction didn't seem to want to end and Kelsie suspected Anna could be almost ready for second stage. It seemed they'd need Connor after all. She doubted they'd make a hospital unless there was one beside the railway track and around the next bend. She could manage the actual birth but wanted someone else here in case the baby did something out of the ordinary.

There was a knock at the door and Kelsie stood up

to open it. Wolfgang's hat was skew and his top button undone.

'I need you to find Dr Black. Is the train anywhere near a hospital? Anna is having a baby.'

Wolfgang looked more horrified than worried for Anna. '*Mon Dieu*. My seats. The carpet.'

'We'll try to be as clean as we can,' Kelsie said dryly. 'Or you could get the doctor and maybe Anna off the train.'

Wolfgang nodded frantically. 'Of course. At once.' He wrung his hands, spun back to her as if to ask another question, and then spun away again to hurry off in the direction of the front of the train.

Kelsie shook her head. She never could understand why people went strange when babies were coming. Surely he knew it was too late now to wish it away. Best to just deal with what came and worry about it later, she thought prosaically.

Anna was breathing heavily again and this time, at the end of the long contraction, Kelsie heard the little catch and hold of breath that signalled the change to second stage.

Uh-oh! Kelsie glanced around the compartment, swept the towel from the hidden wash stand table and rested it on the ridged oil heater against the window to warm. At least she could have something to dry the baby, if nothing else.

The most important thing was to keep the baby warm, after the carpets, she thought wryly to herself.

Anna's nightgown had tiny buttons all the way down the front. It would do. 'You'll have to take off your knickers. Panties.' Anna looked helplessly at Kelsie.

'Underclothes.' Kelsie pretended to pull off her underpants.

She had a horrible thought that surely Anna knew where babies came from? It seemed she did when comprehension flitted across the girl's face. A small mercy.

Another contraction arrived just as she accompanied this feat with huge modesty and this time Anna's expulsive breath frightened both of them.

'What is happening?'

'Your baby is getting ready to come.'

'But it cannot. We are not yet in Paris.'

'Not sure that mindset did much for you not being pregnant either,' Kelsie muttered, and bumped her elbow painfully on a wall. 'These cabins are pathetically small.' She'd bet Connor and his grandmother had a double suite each.

She shifted the pillow from the door side of the bed to the window end. If Anna lay down again the table would be a problem to access and she might just need some room.

Anna moaned just as Wolfgang arrived back with a plastic sheet and two raincoats. Kelsie refused to take them as she helped Anna to breathe calmly.

'Where is Dr Black?' she shot over her shoulder.

'Coming.' Wolfgang thrust the first raincoat at her. 'For the bed,' he implored.

'Okay.' Kelsie glanced at the distraught man. 'We need you somewhere more comfortable, Anna. Do you want to stand up? You might find the contractions easier to bear if you work with them.'

Anna shook her head doubtfully. 'I don't want to move.'

'Do you have pain in your back?' Kelsie asked patiently.

Instinctively Anna's hand went to the small curve in her spine. 'Oh, yes.'

'Then standing will help that and also help your baby to present the easiest way for your birth.'

'Oh. I see.' She struggled to her feet with Kelsie's help, and Kelsie slid the raincoat under the blankets to protect the seats while she was up. Anna stayed doubled over, leaning on the tiny table, as the next pain arrived, but she was listening to Kelsie's instructions.

The young woman seemed to have found an inner calm that Kelsie hadn't expected, though she shouldn't have been surprised—women continued to amaze her all the time in her work. 'You are doing so well. Wonderful.'

'I feel less frightened,' Anna whispered, and Kelsie patted her arm.

With the contraction easing, Kelsie urged Anna to straighten her back into the full upright position before the contraction rolled on, and a sudden startled expression appeared on the girl's face as a thin trickle of pink water ran down her leg and onto the blue carpet in a growing puddle.

Kelsie shot an amused glance at Wolfgang, who gasped in horror then looked at her accusingly, before all the blood slowly drained from his face and he crumpled to his knees in a dead faint, blocking the corridor.

CHAPTER EIGHT

'WHAT IS GOING on here?' The voice of authority arrived before the face did, and Kelsie gave Connor a cool glance as he poked his head around the door as much as he could without stepping on the unconscious Wolfgang.

Kelsie frowned at him. The last thing they needed here were loud voices.

'Anna is having her baby,' she said matter-of-factly. 'You are here in case I need a hand.'

His eyebrows shot up but his voice was low. Teasing. 'Shouldn't you be the one giving me the hand?'

She raised her own brows. 'Catch thirty babies a year, do you?'

'More than you've had breakfasts.' He grinned. 'But I can be your support person.'

The past shimmered between them and the tension lessened in the tiny cabin as they both smiled. It seemed Connor didn't have control issues about this and the thought warmed as well as reassured her.

Connor was about to step over Wolfgang when he changed his mind. 'Give me a minute while Max helps me move our sleeping friend.'

Kelsie looked up from rubbing Anna's back and saw

a tall, distinguished-looking older gentleman nod before he turned away.

Wolfgang moaned and tried to sit up. His eyes rolled towards the much larger puddle on his immaculate blue carpet and then he slumped unconscious again.

Then, bizarrely, Wolfgang's head dragged along the carpet with little bumps as Connor and the boutique manager pulled him unceremoniously out of the doorway by the ankles and he disappeared from view.

Connor stepped back to the now unimpeded doorway. He raised one dark eyebrow. 'Status?'

'Anna's been having contractions since Venice, due date not known, no medical care, on the way to her unsuspecting baby's father in Paris. Her waters broke three minutes ago...' she gestured to the puddle '...much to Wolfgang's dismay, and I think we're almost ready to push.'

'Succinct.' Connor couldn't help admire the calm way Kelsie had managed the transfer of information. And the situation. He saw her glance with a measuring look at Anna. 'I haven't been able to assess the position of the baby.'

Their eyes met and he nodded and tried not to look at the wrong woman because Kelsie's blue gown was knotted at the waist and the soft swell of breast could be seen between the folds.

He looked away to her face and couldn't help thinking she looked so different from the soft and languorous woman he'd left an hour ago. She still looked amazing but there was decision and assurance in every line of her body.

Back on task, he reminded himself. 'We'll assume this baby knows the rules.' He turned to someone behind him. 'Can we get another light, please, Max? Or even a torch in case we need it.'

Connor glanced back along the corridor as the man hurried away. 'Max has seen a lot on this train in the last twenty years,' he said to Kelsie, but didn't mention that apparently that included flirting with his grandmother if the interrupted conversation they'd been having had been what he'd thought it was.

Anna breathed through another contraction and the subtle expulsive effort confirmed Kelsie's diagnosis. He would be right up there with agreeing with her assessment of the situation.

Kelsie looked up when the contraction had eased. 'Do you have a doctor's bag?'

He smiled wryly. 'I'm not the sort of doctor who carries a bag to catch babies away from hospitals.' He shrugged. 'So what have we got on the plus side?'

'Catching babies outside hospitals is right up my alley. And there's two of us.'

He felt his mouth curve. Working with Kelsie was different from what he was used to. 'Great pluses.'

She went on as if ticking off the points. 'Anna is focused and healthy, so baby should be healthy too. And at least it's warm in here.'

All good points. 'So what can I do to help?'

'I need you to take the baby if needed. Get your helper to find us some cord for tying off and scissors to cut the cord. And maybe a dish or a bag for the afterbirth.'

He nodded and spoke to the other porter, who was helping poor Wolfgang to sit up and then turned back to see if he could do anything else.

Kelsie had that far-away look in her eyes that he'd

seen in midwives who could almost disappear in a room they became so unobtrusive, only to soothingly reappear when the woman needed them.

He waited until she refocused and passed her requested items across, and she put them on the small table by the window.

She looked back at him and smiled as if she was very glad he was there. He was conscious that his whole chest seemed to swell. What was it about this woman that touched him so much? Whatever it was, he'd better work out how to put up a force field or he'd be standing outside a registry office on his own again.

'Thank you. That's lovely.' Her voice was soft. 'I can concentrate on Anna. We don't have anything if she decides to bleed, though, but there's no reason she should.'

Connor wondered if she'd said that for Anna's benefit, his benefit or her own. So he agreed in case she needed reassurance. 'Of course she should be fine.'

It all happened very quickly after that. Anna was still standing when Kelsie peered under the hem of the nightgown, much to Anna's embarrassment.

Kelsie murmured, 'So, it is a breech. I wondered. We have our first tiny foot, and now the second has appeared.'

Trickier, Connor thought, but not a disaster, especially if Kelsie was right and both feet had come down together.

He kept his voice low and matter-of-fact, a mirror of Kelsie's, so they didn't alarm the mother. 'Of course it is. Nothing straightforward about a baby that wants to be born on a train.' He lowered his voice even further so that only Kelsie heard. 'Do you want to swap places?'

Kelsie thought about that and appreciated he'd given her the choice. She liked that. But now the birth was a little more complicated he was the more experienced here and they both knew it. She'd delivered a breech birth before but this was no time for glory and not the place to practise.

'Maybe.'

He slid in behind her and she edged away to allow him past so that he was in front of Anna. Kelsie took the towel to dry the baby after birth and spoke in Anna's ear. 'The doctor is taking over now. Everything is fine.'

Anna nodded, too intent on the overwhelming sensations to care, as her uterus contracted again and her baby shifted.

Connor looked up at Kelsie. His voice still low and slightly amused. 'I know what you midwives are like. Don't worry. I'm an advocate for breech babies knowing what they want to do without my interference, too.' He held up his fingers. 'So I'm keeping my hands off.'

Kelsie felt a glow of relief, and pride, and confidence. This was Connor, her Connor, and he'd matured into a caring and skilled man. Maybe he had even recovered from some of his control issues, she thought with a smile, and couldn't help wondering what the future held for them. For the first time she wondered if some time in the future they might even meet again. She hoped so.

He spoke gently to Anna. 'If you can stand the change, it would help if you were to sit on the edge of the seat, Anna. Right near the edge so baby's toes can dangle. We won't lift your skirt until we need to.'

Kelsie slid one of Wolfgang's raincoats onto the floor and Connor knelt beside Anna. The girl's eyes were closed and she was muttering prayers under her breath in an unending litany.

Kelsie decided that was as good as anything to do in the circumstances but everything seemed to be progressing normally—or normal for a breech baby wanting to be born on the Orient Express between countries.

With Anna's change in position her baby's little legs descended further until his hips were suddenly exposed and Connor folded back the nightgown so they could see the progress of the baby. Things would happen faster now.

Anna was having a son. Neither Kelsie nor Connor mentioned it, with the mother concentrating so deeply.

'If the hips fit, the head fits,' Connor said quietly, and Kelsie smiled at him.

'I hadn't heard that before. Very nice.'

Anna's eyes were closed and Max was standing outside the door, available but not observing.

Kelsie leaned out the door and spoke in an undertone. 'Can I get another couple of towels, please, Max?'

He nodded and disappeared up the corridor, returning in less than a minute with warmed towels.

'Impressive.' Kelsie smiled at him before laying one across Connor's knees for him to use if he wanted to wrap baby before it was born.

The descent of the baby continued smoothly, with the help of gravity and his mother bearing down, and Connor's knowledge to keep his hands off a breech baby in case he startled it or pulled, in which case a baby would throw up its head into an alert position, instead of being curled for birth.

Frightened babies ran into problems. It seemed Connor knew that. Kelsie knew that. Some less up-to-date accouchiers didn't know that.

Connor also knew that breech babies could be a little more dazed and reluctant to breathe than babies who came head first. His main concern in this scenario.

So he was much happier to be the catcher to hand the baby on to Kelsie for assessment because he was more used to having a paediatric registrar do all his baby resuscitation while he cared for the woman.

In Kelsie's working world, caseload midwives who caught babies in homes were often in pairs and the second person was always responsible for encouraging reluctant babies to breathe.

Anna's baby had turned a pale shade of blue by the time the head finally arrived and Connor handed the floppy little boy across to Kelsie while he waited for the next stage with the mother.

Kelsie took the limp little body, wiped him quite firmly with a towel, dried him all over so that his little arms wobbled, but after another few seconds a mewling cry was heard, much to Connor's relief.

He watched the mother seem to wake from her stupor at the sound, shake her head and focus on her infant. Then with a gasp she reached for her son, and with the cord still attached he was gently eased into the open front of her gown against her skin.

Anna's son lay with his head on the gentle swell of his mother's breasts, facing Kelsie, so they could see the colour of his face and as he cried with gradually increasing indignation, suddenly pink-cheeked and vigorous.

These were the moments Connor savoured. And judging by the soft look on Kelsie's face, she did too.

He wondered if she regretted not having had babies and then pushed the thought away. Pushed away the concept of a fifteen-year-old child they could have shared because the thought tore at somewhere deep within him.

He returned to the job at hand as the final stage of birth was completed with no damage.

He could hear Anna murmur in Italian, saw out of the corner of his vision the mother stroke the dark fuzz on the baby's head, and then Kelsie tucked another warm towel over them both.

She caught his eye. She'd always caught his eye. This time she held it and for a moment they connected with the satisfaction of a wonderful outcome.

A special moment. Then she sent him a long relieved look and he was surprised because he hadn't realised the depth of her anxiety, but she allowed it to escape now the crisis had passed. Suddenly he wanted to hold her in his arms and reassure her that everything was fine. That she was amazing. But he didn't.

It was one a.m. on Christmas Eve and a baby was born.

Kelsie was the first to speak. 'Congratulations, Anna. He's beautiful.'

'A boy?' The new mother raised tearstained eyes and nodded as the knowledge sank in. 'I cannot believe he is here.'

Over the next sixty minutes tiny Josef had been nursed, dressed in a hand-towel nappy, and clothed in a signature bear outfit from the boutique, so amusingly he looked like Wolfgang in miniature, complete with little blue cap. A tiny naked brown teddy bear sat beside him.

Now sated and wrapped in an Orient Express cash-
mere scarf donated by Max and settled with his mother
after another feed, he was a contented baby.

Wolfgang had recovered, apologised for his unpro-
fessional fainting attack and hastened to offer refresh-
ments, but Max had taken over his duties and sent him
off to sleep.

Anna was clean and warm, pleasantly drowsy and
tucked into the narrow little bed with her baby. Already
she'd spoken to her at first shocked then ecstatic boyfriend on Connor's phone.

A doting waitress had been allocated to sit with the
new mother as she rested, until they arrived in Paris in
the morning, where she and her baby would alight. Kelsie had promised to drop in before they disembarked.

Connor had left instructions for them to wake him
through the night if needed so all bases had been covered.

They'd both washed in the tiny basin in Kelsie's room
and Connor took Kelsie gently by the arm and steered
her back to the bar car, where Max had procured them
a pot of tea.

Max smiled and went on his way, ensuring all was
back to normal on the Orient Express.

Suddenly they were alone on the long settee in the
bar car and Kelsie watched Connor flop back in the seat.

She had to smile as he said with disgust, 'Moments
of unusual interest. Babies!'

Kelsie put her head on his shoulder. 'Such are the
dear wee things. You were awesome.'

'And you were incredible.' He leant her way and
stroked her cheek and she felt like drowsily turning her

mouth to his hand and kissing his palm, but she wasn't sure of her reception after the way they'd parted earlier. He might think she was jumping him again. Seemed she was still a coward.

Instead she said, 'So we have a mutual admiration society. Sounds good to me.'

She closed her eyes for a moment as she nestled beside him on the long couch. Not a night she would forget in a hurry. Then she forced her eyes open and sipped the tea. 'As good as this is, I think I'm too tired to drink it.'

She heard him pick up his cup and then a long swallow. Felt him move his head, as if realising the time. Funny how little things like that made him seem more real. As if them meeting like this had a purpose. Another long draught of his tea and he put his white and blue cup down. 'Then let's get you to bed.'

Ha. Kelsie pouted. 'It didn't work for me last time,' she murmured.

He smiled, put out his hand and pulled her into a standing position. 'You can't have everything you want.'

'What did you say?' she whispered as they crept along the darkened corridor.

She didn't think he would come in when she offered but he did. When her compartment door shut behind them she felt like giggling, but surely Anna and the waitress would hear her if she did.

'I should just kiss you and go,' Connor said very softly.

'I can do that without noise,' she whispered against his mouth, and she could feel his smile against his lips.

CHAPTER NINE

KISSING CONNOR WAS like diving into a hot whirlpool. Again.

Despite both their efforts to cool their ardour, their kiss deepened into something more after the tension and stress of Josef's arrival and the awareness already between them, until Kelsie surrendered to it...and to Connor.

In fact, it deepened into something that the joining of their mouths couldn't satisfy, and her hands began to seek, his followed and both their clothes became disarrayed, all silent flutters of their fingers but no less intense as the dramatic emotion of the night mixed with the unsatisfied emotion of the time before that.

Now it culminated in a flurry of silent desperation as both of them were touched by the past and then lost in the present, in a small swaying cabin in the dark as the snow fell outside.

Until Kelsie stood within the circle of his arms, her once tied dressing gown not designed for resistance, open to the waist as Connor feasted on the bounty within—and she had Connor's shirt pushed aside, baring his chest, her eyes shut, head thrown back. Still with her eyes shut, grinding her teeth as his tongue circled her, while her hands slid across the inflexible muscles of his upper abdomen. Her fingers grazed the pebbled nubs of his nipples, travelled over his taut back and her body arched helplessly against the iron hardness of him and the onslaught of his mouth.

Belts undone, underwear discarded and suddenly everything slowed again and the remaining clothes were lost.

Time itself stopped as they gazed into each other's eyes, and in the background, intermittently, the lights from railway crossings painted them red and then green—and then silver in the snow light while they held each other tight.

Then he sank to sit on the bed, pulled her to kneel between his knees, spanned her waist with his long slender fingers, and inexorably pulled her closer.

This was a Connor she hadn't seen. Grey eyes dark and burning into hers, his hands and mouth sure and possessive, no hurry but no hesitation in steering them to the conclusion neither of them could now contemplate avoiding as she sank downwards.

They both gasped as she lowered, teased, hovered until Connor's hands tightened and she was brought inexorably onto him—all with the sway of the train—a slow and exultant joining, and together they scaled their own mountain as the train sped on through the night.

Afterwards, Connor lay stunned by the storm that had erupted between them, overwhelmed by the connection with the woman he'd always loved. But where was his clarity and responsibility and plain good sense? That was the very core of his mantra to remain in control of his world. That litany had kept him sane from a time when everything had seemed lost at a very young age.

Kelsie made him lose that essential part of his being. Nobody else did. Reason and logic went out the window when he was around her. Look at the fiasco it had been when he'd tried to marry her as a teenager.

He should have been thankful one of them had had the good sense to back away if this tornado was what happened.

And now, when he was far too old to behave like an impulsive, libido-driven teen, he had used no protection. Let alone that he was too well known across Europe to go creeping around train carriages at night for assignations with beautiful midwives.

He couldn't bear the thought of a newspaper story on Kelsie, and already there was a risk of one of the passengers noticing with the obvious rumours of a baby having been born.

God, he was a fool. But first he needed to sort the contraception. All the while in the back of his head a voice was saying that none of those things mattered. He just wanted to lose himself again. And again. And what if he was lost in this and she wasn't!

Sandwiched together in Kelsie's tiny bed, her head on his chest, Kelsie lay in stunned disbelief. She squeezed the strong fingers curled in hers and for the first time she understood why she had never been able to fall in love. Why there had never been any magic with other men.

Connor.

The deep, protected core of her heart had always belonged to the boy she remembered and now this gorgeous, sexy, fabulous man.

She snuggled in further, felt the glow that surrounded them both, and knew she would never be the same.

She was a different person from the woman who had stepped in such a carefree way onto this train from the canals of Venice.

The problem now was that she felt the fragility of finding something so special. That awareness of the rise and fall of the precious chest beneath her cheek and even the flutter of fear should the day come when it would disappear. How crazy was that?

It was as if a huge beacon of light had finally been switched on and she danced like a wraith in the glow. She'd given up long ago thinking that she would feel this way—had, in fact, felt quite proud she was immune to being dependent on a man for happiness.

Now she just wanted to lose herself in his eyes again, see the man she could finally admit could be the one to spend her life with, but it was too hard with her nose buried in his chest.

Her brain began to function again and with it came fear. Would she lose this, too?

They didn't have long but they had some time when they arrived in London. Not much chance of a future with them on opposite sides of the world but that was for later.

No hurry, the rational part of herself reminded her, they wouldn't arrive until late in the afternoon. She should just savour this moment for as long as she could. Maybe even till dawn. Or was she just imagining he felt the same?

Fear gnawed away at her. She needed to know Connor's thoughts and turned her head but couldn't see his face from this angle. He was strangely silent, though he held her in their tiny cocoon.

Finally she had to probe. Quietly. 'Are you okay?'

His hand tightened. She heard the smile in his voice when he answered. 'I'm supposed to ask you that.'

She stretched her toes and rubbed his ankle under the sheets. 'I'm feeling wonderful.'

'I'm glad. But we have to talk.'

She snuggled in. About...? And waited with anticipation. Christmas in London? They'd already discussed the past. Was it time to talk about the future?

'The train stops for almost an hour in Paris. I'll get off and find an all-night chemist. They'll have a morning-after pill. I can't believe I didn't use protection. I'm sorry. It's inexcusable.'

What? She blinked and her head lifted a few millimetres off his chest.

That's what he was thinking? What? Poor little Kelsie needed safeguarding from the big bad man without protection? Or maybe he was worried that she'd trap him! As in the opposite to dropping him fifteen years ago? Did he think she cruised through life unprepared?

Not what she'd expected to hear. Maybe because she'd known she was covered pregnancy-wise but he hadn't even asked that.

Apparently she was still too silly not to have thought of contraception.

I'm on the Pill, she shrilled at him silently. And as for the other concerns she didn't think that, no matter how much he'd changed, Connor was the kind of man to give a sleeping partner a notifiable disease. Well, neither was she.

It was disquieting the way his mind worked, though. Did he trust her so little? Was he that worried about unwanted complications? Was that finally the price she would pay for her actions in the past?

Did he think she would escape in London and not follow through? Did he want to ensure all was settled before they parted?

Her bubble of euphoria deflated and disappeared like suds down a porcelain bowl onto railway tracks and she sat up. Slid from the bed and picked up her robe.

'You okay?' he asked.

Umm. No. But she didn't say anything. Slipped the robe on and belted it before she turned to face him. Saw the closed look on his face and tried to keep her own expression blank as she wondered how she could escape so she could figure this out by herself.

She poked her feet into her slippers and unlatched the door. 'Excuse me.' Smiled in his general direction and fled.

Connor jammed his fingers through his hair.

He'd truly lost it. Their lovemaking had been torrid. The last thing he wanted was Kelsie finding out in a month she was pregnant and he'd ruined her life. Especially if this was only a one-night stand for her.

He pushed away the stupid idea that he could live with the incredible idea of Kelsie having his child.

A child? Imagine if she left him then!

He shuddered. He wasn't doing wives and children and family who could leave at any time. He needed to put his trust in his work. It was his job to make sure other people had families.

He slid from the bed and began to dress before she came back, though he doubted even his grandmother would rouse the train to look for him—though she hadn't worried about shocking him when she'd sent Max in to talk to him.

He hadn't even had time to digest that startling turn of events in the last crazy few hours. But he had his own dilemmas now.

Kelsie still wasn't back as he shrugged into his jacket, the better to hide his crumpled shirt he'd rescued from the floor—he couldn't believe he hadn't hung it up!—and he straightened his tie and checked his phone.

Looked again. 'Please call urgently.' Damn. The Wilsons. Another baby in danger. He highlighted the number and opened Kelsie's door but she wasn't in the corridor.

He couldn't phone here, with people sleeping in every cabin, and he moved swiftly in the opposite direction until finally he reached the dimly lit bar car and could phone without fear of disturbing others.

He listened to a tearful Connie beg him to call and reassured himself that of all people Kelsie would understand when a mother needed him. Ignored the thought that flitted through his mind that he couldn't wait to get back to a situation in which he had some rules to follow. Because he was damned if knew what the rules were with Kelsie. He dialed the Wilsons' number.

When Kelsie came back from the bathroom he'd gone. She'd thought he might have.

Her shoulders drooped and she shut the door and locked it. Hadn't she been the biggest goose. All soft and squishy over the old boyfriend and he had just been there for the night. Thank goodness she hadn't said anything to reveal her feelings. But inside she was shrivelling.

Mourning the silly dream she'd indulged in when he'd never said anything about tomorrow. Thanked her stars it wasn't a ten-night train journey or it could have been really embarrassing.

But it was a one-night journey. Breakfast would be served in the cabin in four or five hours. She wouldn't even see him. Then would be the pause in Paris, when she'd say goodbye to Anna and Josef, and hopefully meet the new father and make sure all was fine.

Then no doubt she'd see Connor at that point, because he'd drop in her little parcel containing the morning-after pill.

She narrowed her eyes at that. Toyed with idea of saying, 'No need, I'm covered,' but decided against it. Let him tramp about Paris at six a.m. and find a pharmacy because she wasn't feeling charitable about that one.

She climbed back into bed and pulled the second pillow over her head so she could hide. Didn't hear the quiet knock as it came at her door. Or hear Connor walk away.

Oblivious, Kelsie was sternly analysing recent events. Did she regret that she'd seen and lost Connor again?

No, she couldn't. She'd had the chance to say her

piece. Explain a little and apologise for the past. Something she'd wanted to do for a long time.

Did she regret meeting his grandmother—the actual woman who had inspired her dream of travelling on the Orient Express? No way!

Was she unhappy she'd opened herself to Connor more than she had to any man? It had been special! She wasn't believing anything else. So how could she regret that?

No regret in learning what amazing sex was, finally, despite the mortifying ending. No. And it wasn't so humiliating when only she had known how much it had affected her.

Stern talking to completed, she shifted the pillow from her head and hugged it. Tried not to notice the faint scent of his cologne, breathed slowly in and out until her body reminded her it was very tired, but she couldn't sleep. Eventually the clack of the rails lulled her and the next thing she knew it was dawn.

Or a slow increase of dawn. In the dim light as she peered through heavy eyes the window began to expose the houses, see the waking city on the outskirts of Paris, the flash of a waterway between houses and a tiny curved bridge reminiscent of Venice twenty hours ago.

With the dawn they rattled closer and closer to Paris and Kelsie washed her face, dressed and unsnapped her privacy catch as the train slowed for the pause on the outskirts before they rolled into the station. What would she give for a hot cup of tea?

There was a knock at the door and, magically, Wolfgang was there, looking sheepish, holding her dream tray with steaming water and an array of teabags.

'I was told you wanted to see the young lady and her baby off the train.' His cheeks reddened. 'I wish also to apologise for my odd behaviour. I do appreciate all your help last night.'

'Wolfgang. You darling. You were fine. And thank you for this.' She took the tray and then hesitated, hadn't been going to ask but couldn't help herself. 'Is Dr Black going to see Anna off as well?'

'I believe Dr Black has already seen them, madam.'

How had she missed that commotion through the thin walls? 'Oh. Then I will too, as soon as I've had this.'

Stepping back onto the train after seeing Anna and tiny Josef tucked into a taxi outside the station, Kelsie felt at least one family was happy.

They'd headed off at Anna's boyfriend's insistence for the hospital to be thoroughly checked out before he took them home to his flat. Though she did wonder what the Venetian grandparents were going to say about their new grandchild's unexpected arrival.

Anna's compartment door was shut and no doubt Wolfgang was planning a huge spring clean. The thought made her smile, which was a good thing considering the fact that Connor had run far and fast as soon as he'd dropped her little package in her compartment while she'd been gone.

She picked it up, curled her lip and tossed it in the tiny waste receptacle. She hoped he'd had the devil's own time finding it.

Her own little bed had been packed up and the seat had been returned to the daytime configuration. She decided the least she could do was enjoy the rest of her trip. She needed to remember that was why she was here.

Breakfast arrived and Wolfgang placed the flower-decorated tray on her tiny table in front of the window.

The train still sat in the Paris station awaiting clear-ance. Above her head cars and pedestrians streamed past in the peak-hour traffic, and the world went on turning while she waited in solitary splendour in her compartment.

She glanced down at the food. Fruit salad, pastries and rolls, wonderful jams to choose from, deliciously evil curled balls of French butter, and freshly squeezed juice. Far too much for one person—especially one who didn't appreciate them. She resisted the urge to push it all away crossly as she thought about Connor and her inability to understand him.

She picked at the food as she watched the passers-by scurry along the streets of Paris from her stationary train carriage, watched the buses fly over the overpass, and thought that soon she would be one of those hurry-ing off to work herself.

When she was back in the real world. The world she'd worked so hard to create for herself.

But that was for later.

After Christmas.

It was Christmas Eve, she reminded herself, and she would be in London later today, across the world from her home, and booked in at the Ritz for Christ-mas morning before she left for the airport. It had all seemed so exciting when she'd looked at her itinerary before she'd left.

At the moment it looked a little flat and she chided herself for being pathetic. She needed to work on that.

CHAPTER TEN

CONNOR SAT IN the large double cabin facing his grandmother, his head in a medical journal as he tried to catch up on the latest breakthroughs in fertility. There were two articles with his name to them in the current issue and he needed to check that they had been presented correctly.

But his mind was elsewhere. Not with the Wilsons, because that had been a false alarm, though he suspected labour could be drawing closer for them, but hopefully not until after he and his grandmother arrived in London. Hopefully, also, when his brain was less scattered.

His short opportunity for sleep and the lack of rest it had provided didn't help.

Partly because of the recurring dream, the one he hadn't had for several years now. It was always the same, the horror of light dying from eyes fixed on his, and he'd woken before dawn, heart pounding and in a lather of sweat, and had known fear like he hadn't for years.

Desperately disappointed at its return, because he'd hoped the nightmare had finally been banished, this time instead of his mother's face the woman's face had been in shadow—and yet he'd known it was Kelsie, even though he hadn't been able to see her features.

God, he hated the power of dreams that could strike terror into his psyche when he was at his weakest. No control to be had there.

One of the reasons he'd never seriously contemplated even a sensible marriage, or stayed the night at any of his women friends' homes, was his horror of anyone finding out about this little weakness. He doubted anyone knew he suffered those dreams except his grandmother, who had caught him at a weak moment years ago when he'd been staying over and she'd heard him cry out. That moment still made him cringe.

This morning the nightmare had receded to an eerily distant threat, so much so that it still clouded his thoughts, which were already in disarray with his angst about Kelsie. Why hadn't she answered the door when he'd gone back? Had she been soundly asleep—or deliberately avoiding him?

He hadn't tried again when he'd been to see Anna and Josef early that morning in case she was still sleeping. At least that visit had been successful and both seemed unfazed by the baby's unusual arrival. Good to see someone was happy.

He'd written a referral to a medical colleague in one of the maternity hospitals in Paris for a follow-up visit.

But still the dilemma of Kelsie lingered. His eyes stared unfocused on the page.

Ah, Kelsie. The memories of that morning were still very vivid in his mind. Her glorious body, her ability to tilt his world and spin it until he didn't know which way was up, the woman who could explore deeply sheltered parts of him that nobody else had access to. He hated that. Was terrified of it. Loved it.

So much so that he wondered if that was where the dream had come from.

He'd have to try and talk to her again. Try to understand what she was thinking. He'd always wished she'd let him into her thoughts more. He'd ruined the mood disastrously by talking about the morning-after pill. Maybe the idea of repercussions had been just as terrifying for her as it had been for him but second-guessing her was difficult.

He'd been unable to settle ever since he'd returned to meet his grandmother for breakfast.

'You're very quiet.' Winsome sounded bored and he put his journal down. Hadn't been reading the thing anyway.

Poor Gran. He was not good company this morning because all he could think about was the impact he was already feeling after the time with Kelsie. He suspected she was about to fly back to Australia and out of his life once again.

'Sorry. What would you like to talk about?'

'You won't like what I want to talk about.'

He smiled. She was probably right. 'Thankfully it's not your pseudo-birthday any more now it's Christmas Eve. So you have to spare me.'

She pouted and he grinned. 'Don't try your wiles on me. You're not talking to Max now, Gran.'

She smiled at that. 'He is a darling. Are you sure you don't mind?'

'Of course I don't. He seems a good fellow. But that's none of my business.' And she was safely diverted to another topic for the next fifteen minutes, and Connor hoped she'd take the staying-out-of-each-other's-business hint on board.

He'd got over the shock of his eighty-year-old grandmother finding companionable love and truly appreciated the benefits to her not living alone as she grew older. He had the feeling the two elderly lovebirds wouldn't waste much time sorting out their future arrangements.

Lucky them.

Shame he didn't believe the same could happen to him but with that thought came his resolution to find Kelsie and try to understand where they could possibly go with this—if, indeed, there was anywhere to go.

Kelsie was sick of her own company but trapped in the dilemma of not running into Connor somewhere on the train if she ventured out of her cabin. The last thing she wanted was to look like she was chasing him.

When Wolfgang came to remove her tray she pounced on him and, despite the risk of looking needy, she encouraged his continued presence.

'So what's on the agenda for today, Wolfgang?'

He bowed. 'A delicious brunch will be served in the dining car, madam, at eleven.'

Her stomach groaned. More food. 'In case I was starving to death by now.' She nodded and Wolfgang looked slightly confused.

'I'm sorry. Not enough sleep for me.' He nodded and looked slightly guilty again so she hurried on. 'And what time do we arrive in Calais?'

'Around one o'clock in Calais. The Ville coaches

will transfer you to the shuttle terminal at Coquelles. Then through the tunnel to Folkestone where, after a short wait, you will join the Pullman train for the journey to London.' He smiled at her. 'There will be a very elegant afternoon tea on that train.'

She grinned back. 'Of course there will. I will be as big as a house by the time I get off at Victoria. So we lose you at Calais?'

He bowed. 'Our hostesses will accompany each VIP coach and hand you on to the new Pullman Stewards.'

She'd miss him. Had enjoyed his blue-suited attentiveness and his staid good humour. 'Thank you for explaining that. I guess I thought we caught this train all through the tunnel to London.'

Horrified that 'his' train would go across the Channel, he exclaimed, 'No! No! It is the Pullman train you will transfer to for the final leg.'

There was something sad in that. She liked her blue wagon lit. 'I understand. So when we all leave you will go home for Christmas?'

He smiled. 'Yes. We all go home. It is the last trip of the year. Normally our timetable finishes much earlier but this trip had been rescheduled so it became a special journey.'

Lucky her. 'I feel very fortunate. So you're on holidays now?'

He nodded and she wondered vaguely how his hat stayed on with all his nodding and bowing.

Oblivious to her curiosity, he went on, 'All except those who have other employment. VSOE have many hotels and we can move between them if we wish.'

'I hope your Christmas is delightful, Wolfgang,

though I'm sure I'll see you before I go. You do a fabulous job of looking after us.'

He bowed, hat still amazingly glued on. 'Thank you.' He gestured towards the front of the train. 'The bar car is open if you wish to change scenery.'

'Sounds good, but I think I'll try and get to the boutique again to buy something to remind me of my journey. I didn't make it yesterday.' And she doubted Connor would be hanging out in there again today just in case she turned up.

Wolfgang went on his way and Kelsie dug out her purse for a walk through the train. The bar car was filling up and she wondered if she'd manage to find a seat when she came back through again. It was still early and she wondered where Winsome was or if she was still asleep.

The boutique was the last carriage before the engine. Apart from Max, it was deserted.

'Miss Summers. Welcome.' So he remembered her when she wasn't dressed in her pyjamas. She smiled and could picture how unobtrusively helpful he'd been. He didn't look as though he'd been up all night. Still immaculate, distinguished, his Italian accent rolled velvety and vibrantly and his chocolate-brown eyes were warm with welcome.

'Max, isn't it? Dr Black said you'd seen a lot in the last twenty years on the Orient Express. You were very good last night.'

He bowed. No hat to keep on. 'It is you who were excellent. But I enjoy people and the drama of the journey.'

She thought a breech birth on a train did justify the

description. 'Well, we certainly had drama last night. That's for sure.'

Max nodded. 'I believe that is our first baby born on board.'

Kelsie laughed, picturing the scene. 'Josef looked so cute afterwards when he was dressed in the little conductor suit.' She looked at the teddy bears, all dressed as Josef had been, and then at the more exotic gifts like cuff links, VSOE diamond bracelets and gorgeous pearl drop sets. 'I bet you've seen some romance here as well.'

She actually thought he blushed. She wasn't sure because he went on in his beautiful accent, as if nothing was a problem, 'This is the train of love. People come time and again. Anniversaries. Weddings.' He gazed into pleasant past. 'I have seen men propose on bended knee in the crowded dining car and then buy expensive and beautiful jewellery from my boutique.' He shrugged with a smile. 'All of this makes me happy.'

Kelsie decided Max was a bit of a honey as well as a romantic as she tried to decide on the perfect memento of her trip.

Footsteps sounded at the door and whoever it was must have been a favourite face because Max's eyes softened and his smile would have lit up the room. Kelsie turned to see Winsome smiling back at him and then the older lady seemed to tear her eyes away to beam at Kelsie.

'Hello, my dear. I thought you might be here. Max's little boutique is the best part of the journey.'

Kelsie wondered at the unmistakably flirtatious note in her voice, and wondered if Connor knew his gran had a thing for Max.

Another footfall and a deep voice. It seemed he did. 'Behave yourself, Gran. You're embarrassing Max.' When Connor entered, the relaxed and festive vibe for Kelsie seemed to be swallowed by the awareness of his powerful presence. And the way his eyes immediately searched for hers.

Max and Winsome didn't seem to notice anything, thank goodness, Kelsie thought as she mentally wrapped herself in a suit of armour to stave off the weakness she could feel creeping around her knees.

'Your beautiful grandmother only ever gives me pleasure,' Max said heroically to the man lounging at the door. Kelsie had to smile at Winsome, who fanned herself theatrically.

Maybe it was time to change the subject. And prove she was no wilting flower just because Connor had skulked away from her bed. 'Max is going to help me decide,' she said to the room in general. 'I'm stuck. So what should I have as a memento for my trip?'

Winsome winked at the manager again. 'Max is very good at that.'

Max bestowed a shake of his head on her but the affection between the two was obvious. So Max had a thing for Winsome as well, Kelsie decided with an internal smile. Well, good on them. Nice if it all worked out for someone.

Max returned his attention to Kelsie. 'Perhaps you could point out those things that appeal to you?' The wave of his hand included the whole display. 'Include those that are outside your price range just for the fun of it.'

She looked around. Carefully avoided Connor at the

door. 'I can't say one of everything because that would be too greedy.'

The crystalware caught her eye as it reflected the light in myriad colours. It would remind her of dinner with Connor, and she would dearly love a set of each of those. 'The engraved crystal glasses. I love them. And the decanter is gorgeous. At least one of the beautiful snuff boxes and of course any of the jewellery, it's all divine.'

She stepped closer to the glass cabinet that held the diamonds and gold. 'I'm particularly fond of the charm bracelet with the tiny train and conductor's hat, and the diamond earrings with matching pendant.' She moved along the cabinet. 'And I should buy one of these beautiful VSOE velvet jewellery rolls to keep it all in.'

She stopped and blushed. 'Lost it for a moment in the daydream.' Shook her head. 'But enough dreaming. I think I would like a silver guard's whistle and an Agatha Christie book. Thank you, Max.'

'Excellent choice,' he said, as he carefully removed the gold-edged book from the pile.

'Only one of a thousand printed in this edition.' He was too much a gentleman to look disappointed she hadn't spent a fortune. 'And the whistle is very popular.' He wrapped them swiftly and elaborately, his vast experience obvious. Then placed her purchases in a little gold VSOE carry-bag, along with a catalogue. 'In case you see something you would like to order online.'

'You are very good at this. Aren't you?'

He nodded complacently.

She could feel Connor observing it all from the door, though he didn't say anything. Couldn't stop herself babbling to fill the awkward pause, though she was probably the only one who felt the awkwardness of the moment. 'So you must be going home for Christmas, too, after we disembark?'

'Actually, I'm not.' He glanced at Winsome. 'I have been invited for Christmas in London. And yourself?'

Kelsie wondered if Connor knew that but he made no demur. What a delightful intrigue. Perhaps more than just a flirtation?

Then she realised Max was waiting for her answer. 'I'm having Christmas morning at the Ritz and then flying back to Australia later tomorrow. I discovered it's incredibly cheap to fly home on Christmas Day.'

Winsome looked horrified. 'Oh, no. You can't go on Christmas night.'

Kelsie smiled gently at the kindness she could see in Winsome's eyes. 'Of course I can. I've worked every Christmas the last few years. It's never really been a big thing for me. This year will be a treat and I get to sit back. Then I'm working every day for a week from New Year's Eve.' She smiled at Max. 'Hoping to catch lots of babies who very kindly waited for me until after Christmas.'

She picked up her carry-bag and smiled vaguely in Connor's direction. 'I'll see you all later.'

She thought she'd got away with it but Connor leaned towards her as she passed.

'I'll accompany you.' Connor turned to follow.

Softly answered into his chest as she passed, 'I'd rather you didn't.'

'Tough,' he said quietly, so that only she could hear. So not like the young man she'd known.

She narrowed her eyes and muttered over her shoulder. 'I can't stop you.'

'No. You can't.' Whispered into her hair.

CHAPTER ELEVEN

WAS HE TRYING to be annoying or just obtuse? Kelsie had to wonder what had happened to the incredibly attentive man who had held her so tenderly after they had both rocked their little cabin, the man who she'd thought had become her lover and a best friend again.

'I'm going to the bar.'

She heard the laughter in his voice. 'Be careful. They'll feed you.'

She stopped, turned, and her mouth twitched. She had to smile. Suddenly it was easier. 'You're overly stuffed with food too?' Maybe he wasn't so over her. Or was hiding it so she would just fall for him all over again with the barest hint of encouragement.

He grimaced. 'I ache with food.'

Actually, Connor ached with something else. The urge to hold Kelsie and hug her to him. Grab her hand and race her off to her cabin—much more private—because this was the last opportunity they would have to be alone before they were transferred to the non-sleeper part of their journey—but that way lay madness. Or was it happiness that he was afraid of?

He wished he knew which it was, although the ghosts

from the past had such a stranglehold on him he had to assume the former.

Now he'd discovered she was flying out tomorrow night they had very little time. He'd been disappointed when that had come out but not shocked. They had less reason to be careful because she would fly away and now he knew. No doubt she would have mentioned it yesterday if he'd asked her.

In fairness to himself, his intention hadn't been to sleep with her and find himself teetering on the edge of where he'd been all those years ago—back under her spell.

Maybe it was a good thing she was going. Not enough time for the miracle of Christmas to take a hand. But they should at least part friends.

He owed her that. He actually thought he needed it, too.

'Perhaps we could talk privately?'

The blue of her eyes darkened doubtfully and he thought again how much he loved the way her face had matured into the woman in front of him.

'Why?'

He shrugged. He wished he knew. 'For lots of reasons—all of them nebulous.' But he couldn't rid himself of the notion that they were balancing on the edge of an important truth—no matter which way it went. 'Or just because I left without explanation this morning and it wasn't my intention to hurt you.'

She shrugged unwillingly. 'We can talk in the bar.'

'Of course.' Kelsie heard the resignation in his voice.

She chewed her lip as she moved forward again through the next carriage. Did she really want to talk in the bar? With Winsome about to descend on them at any moment and the possibility of others overhearing?

Or did she want to risk being in close, private proximity to Connor where physical things could happen? Had happened before. Ooh. Naughty but nice.

She considered her lonely flight home tomorrow, at thirty thousand feet, imagining scenarios in her head if she chose the wrong answer now.

Would she regret not giving him a chance to speak to her in private? Yes. Best not to wonder, then. 'Fine. Your cabin or mine?'

Connor smiled. 'Mine's closer. And larger.'

Her brows went up. She'd known it would be. 'Show-off.'

He looked down at her. 'Jealous bag.'

She laughed. 'You always were good at the comebacks.'

'You weren't too bad yourself when you plucked up the courage.'

'I've grown up,' she tossed over her shoulder.

'Oh, yes,' he said softly. 'You certainly have.'

He touched her shoulder, she stopped, and they were there already. More reasons to go to his cabin. He unlocked his cabin and gestured for her to enter.

'Madam?' He looked so tall as he smiled down at her. So big and achingly familiar, and she could almost taste the impending loss, because they would be a world away from each other very shortly. But that was her life and she loved her life.

She looked up into his face as she passed under his arm and she remembered the last time they had been alone. Felt the twist in her belly and the warmth in her skin as she brushed against him. 'Come into my parlour, said the spider to the fly.'

He shook his head. 'To my mind it's more of a black-widow thing.'

With her being the black widow? Not very complimentary!

He must have seen he'd offended her. Good. 'Let's just say I'm pretty sure you can protect yourself if you want to.'

Ah. But right at this moment did she want to? Kelsie hoped those thoughts didn't show in her face as she looked around the spacious suite. Two large seats facing each other with a table between them. Twice the size of her cabin and at least that much more expensive. She'd never really thought about the financial disparity between them but that reared its head now as another reason a relationship wouldn't work.

'So is this all yours?'

'It connects through that door to my grandmother's suite, which is the same.'

'Nice.'

He crossed to the tiny refrigerator she'd missed in the corner. 'Would you like a cold drink?'

'Juice. Thanks.' Something to do with her hands was always good.

He sat down when they both had drinks. Opposite each other, the air heavy with unspoken thoughts, both with small smiles on their faces as they compared the stilted awkwardness to how they had been just a few hours ago.

Connor started. 'I hope I didn't upset you this morning when I left without saying goodbye—'

Did he expect her to say yes? She interrupted. 'I admit I thought it was a little unusual but I'm not needy.'

Much. She so did not want to be needy. 'So what did you want to talk about?' She paused, thought and then said it out loud. 'Contraception, perhaps?' She wouldn't put it past him and would not get her hopes up it could be something a little more flattering.

'Did you get the package I left?'

Surprise. Surprise. 'Hmm.' Bite your tongue, Kelsie! Say nothing.

He leaned forward. 'So you've taken them.'

'No,' she said coolly, and stood up. She didn't want to do this. She wanted out. Now! 'It makes me angry you're so obsessed with something that isn't your business. I didn't need them because I'm already covered. It's what grown women do.'

He stood too. 'Wait.' Touched her arm, carefully, as if afraid she'd brush him off, his eyes perplexed. 'Why didn't you say so?'

She shrugged. 'Offended mostly. I thought you were very speedy at declaring the risk of not being protected because you were so sure I wasn't.'

Like she was still a silly little girl. Not a mature, professional woman. If she didn't get out of here soon she was going to cry and she did not want to do that! She'd spent the last fifteen years growing up. Growing a tough outer layer. Fighting to be the independent woman she'd thrown away the young Connor to become.

'Okay.' So perhaps it had been a bad choice to leave her like that. 'I'm sorry. But there was other stuff going on.' Connor wanted to pull his hair out. At least she'd finally explained how she felt. Half the time he had no idea what she was thinking and it wasn't surprising he'd managed to upset her.

He thought of telling her about the phone call but knew he'd been glad of the excuse. So that was a cop-out. 'Though, to be fair to me, contraception or lack of it *is* my business. I don't know if you see me as a one-night stand or an old boyfriend but either way the honourable thing to do is ensure you don't become pregnant when I'm the one who's been irresponsible.'

'You've still got control issues.'

He stilled. Stared at her thoughtfully. 'No. You think I have but I don't. I have care issues. I'm beginning to think you're the one with the control problem.'

'That's not true. You're just sexist.' And she spun on her heel and walked out.

Connor looked at the empty doorway. 'Sexist?' He repeated it. 'Me? Sexist?' He adored women. He was a reproductive specialist, for pity's sake, and he respected and admired women immensely.

She had serious trust issues. He knew her parents had been very unhappy before they'd separated; her father had drunk a fair bit and maybe it wasn't about him at all. Maybe she was terrified of falling in love and committing to one person for ever? Well, she wasn't the only one. His phone rang and he turned away from the door and stared unseeingly out the window as he answered it.

Kelsie swept out of his compartment with her cheeks hot but not as hot as her temper. Did he want her to say he wasn't a one-night stand? And why was it all about his honour? He made her so angry but she just couldn't pinpoint why. She'd said the one thing she'd known would alienate him and reminded herself why she hadn't thrown herself on his chest.

As she flounced through the bar car, she decided against any form of male company, ever, and she glared at Winston Whatsit the Third when he stood up and smiled at her until he shrank back in his chair.

His terrified reaction did something to restore her good humour. Yes. That's right. She was a woman to reckon with, wasn't she? A black widow. Thank goodness she didn't need a man to make her feel like she had a perfect life.

When she reached her compartment she resisted the urge to dig out her bottle of limoncello she'd bought as a last-minute impulse in Venice and pour a generous slosh into her glass. *Grrrrr*, she thought as she glared at the bottle made famous in the lemon groves of the Amalfi coast. She'd like to bury someone in the lemon groves on the Amalfi coast.

Connor sat with his grandmother and stuffed his frustration, anger and disappointment in Kelsie into a sealed box somewhere under his diaphragm, where it sat like a lump.

He saw his grandmother open the yellow envelope and then frown across at him. He was in trouble. Well, what was new!

Winsome pointed the paper at him. 'What did you do to that poor girl?'

What had she done to *him* was more like it! 'Which poor girl?'

His gran's eyes almost disappeared as she glared at him and for the first time in half an hour he felt like smiling. 'Don't play with me, Connor. You know I mean Kelsie.'

He couldn't believe he was the one being scolded when he had been the one ill used. The whole thing was the result of two incompatible people butting their heads against a brick wall. But he did hate to see his gran upset. 'Nothing. She's fine.'

The letter was waved his way. 'She's apologised for not joining us for brunch.'

He sat forward. Caught his grandmother's eye and held it. 'That poor girl has been forced into our company the whole trip. She's probably having lunch with Winston Whatsit the Third.'

His grandmother looked a little hurt that he'd suggested she'd forced their company on Kelsie. He saw the pang of guilt cross her face and truly regretted that. But before he could apologise she'd absorbed his next comment.

'Eh? With who? Who's he?' Diversion was always good with Gran. Lowered the blood pressure.

'Fellow at the bar. He fancied her, I think.'

Another death stare. 'And that doesn't bother you?'

Not at all. Kelsie wouldn't touch a man that drank to excess with a ten-foot pole. He knew that much. 'Why should it?'

His grandmother gave her most impressive snort yet. 'Hmmmph! Because you're damn well in love with the girl, that's why.'

The humour abruptly left the conversation.

He was seriously fed up with this whole situation. In fact, thanks to his grandmother and a certain person who would remain nameless, he'd probably acquired a phobia about trains for life!

'Kelsie Summers and I are not meant to be together. That's the end of it.' He stood up. 'I'm going to the bar.'

'Well, I'm going to lunch!'

'I hope you enjoy your brunch, Grandmother,' he said very calmly and quietly. 'I'm afraid I won't be joining you either.'

Kelsie picked at her brunch with a very nice lady who was recovering from cancer and had become a naturopath.

She talked to Heath, the waiter, who had also been born in Sydney, like she had, and a lovely couple who had saved for five years to enjoy the journey on their tenth wedding anniversary. Max must have loved them.

She struggled through fluffy eggs with Scottish salmon, lobster with truffle sauce and a small slice of white Christmas cake with VSOE chocolates on the side.

Oh, my goodness, she thought as she placed her hand protectively over her stomach and put down her silverware.

It wasn't gluttony, it was diversion from not looking through into the next cabin where she could see the back of Winsome's head. Or not searching for the dark one that would be close by.

She was starting to dislike all food. Finally it was time to return to her own compartment and pack the last of her belongings into her shoulder bag before they arrived in Calais.

As she glanced around her snug little cabin she never

would have believed she would be wishing this journey to end, but that was how she felt. And it was all Connor Black's fault.

Finally the train arrived and it was time to transfer from the gorgeous Orient Express, bursting with tradition, opulence and dignified pride, to a coach! How unglamorous was that?

Half a dozen VIP coaches were lined up waiting for them and at the bottom of each set of steps a busy, blue-suited VSOE hostess carried a clipboard and checked off names.

When Kelsie cast a lingering glance back at her previous transport Wolfgang was there lined up in front of the last carriage with the other staff, posing for pictures.

There was Max, looking very distinguished, and the head chef with his towering white chef's hat, and the maître d', black-suited and standing very straight, and Heath the waiter looking a little pink in the cheeks at all the attention, as passengers took photos of the staff.

Kelsie had to smile when she saw Winsome thrust her camera into 'that man's' hands and hurry forward for a photo of her with the official entourage as she squeezed in between Wilhelm and Max. Then she remembered the older lady had said it was her last trip.

Symbolically the end of an era for Winsome— though hopefully it was the beginning of a new spring with her time with Max.

For Kelsie it was just the end of a train journey. She turned away.

Connor took the snap of his gran, and had to smile at her waving him on to take another. It was a good thing he didn't have time to see which coach Kelsie was boarding. As he put the camera down his grandmother came up, beaming, beside him. At least they were coming to the end of this awful train journey where he'd just complicated the blazes out of his life, but despite everything he was truly glad to have seen his grandmother so happy.

His phone vibrated in his pocket and he frowned. Unexpected phone calls rarely heralded good news. 'Excuse me,' he said to Winsome, and answered. Listened. 'I'll ring you back,' he said, and ended the call.

'Gran?'

Winsome gazed around like a kid in a lolly shop, soaking in the moment, a brightness to her eyes that could have been excitement or maybe the shine of tears, and reluctantly she drew her attention back to him.

'I need to head straight to London as quickly as possible for the patients I told you about. The mother is bleeding and they'd like me to be there. Would you be all right if I left now and had you met at Victoria?'

He saw her blink and focus more fully on him. 'Now?'

'They're sending a helicopter for me.'

She frowned. 'Don't like helicopters. I'll take the train.' She glanced at him coyly. 'I can always find Kelsie and sit with her.'

Internal wince. 'Or Lady Geraldine. She'd love your company.' He resisted the impulse to warn her to stay away from Kelsie. But it would only encourage her. 'Would you like me to find Lady G. and Charlotte?'

'No. No. I'll be fine.'

'You're sure?' He looked at her. Her cheeks were overbright and yet the rest of her face was a little pale.

It had been a huge twenty-four hours and she'd had a fair intake of food—and wine! Maybe he shouldn't go?

'Go,' she shooed him. 'Go to that poor woman. I'll be fine. I've been fine for eighty years without you hovering at my elbow. I'll be fine for the next six hours.'

He redialled the number but the whole time he waited for a connection he studied Winsome. She didn't seem to be flagging. Lord, the woman had more energy than he did.

Harry Wilson picked up.

'That's fine. If you send the helicopter I'll come now.'

Gran would be fine. He'd ask Max to find a hostess to watch out for her and arrange for someone to meet her at Victoria. And Nick, Charlotte's fiancé, was a doctor so at least there was medical help on the train if needed.

The Wilsons were his last patients with a baby due this year. His next wasn't due till February. So he could stay longer with Gran afterwards to make up for this.

He spoke to Wolfgang, who nodded, and his bag was identified and handed over and he was directed to a far corner of the car park where a large orange cross was painted on the bitumen.

Apparently it wasn't unusual for passengers to skip the Channel crossing and take a helicopter to London from here.

He didn't have to wait long before the beat of helicopter rotors could be heard, which only increased his respect for Harry Wilson's business arm.

As long as Winsome was okay, this had worked out well. He was glad to get away.

After he'd watched his grandmother helped aboard one of the big silver coaches he'd refused to look for any other people he might know. Specifically one who had labelled him a controlling sexist. No wonder she hadn't married him if she thought that. All he'd ever wanted to do was look after her. What was so heinous about that?

The helicopter drew closer and he cast a last glance across to the coaches. Which one was she on?

No! He was glad he could remove himself from the temptation to do something as monumentally stupid as he'd done all those years ago. It was a good thing.

Ten minutes later, as the helicopter took off he couldn't help but glance down. The train looked like a toy. As did the coaches as they began to pull out of the car park. He glanced ahead and the sky was grey and featureless. Not unlike his life stretching out before him.

CHAPTER TWELVE

KELSIE TURNED AWAY, brushed away the regret that she'd probably never see any of these people again, and made darned sure she was on a different coach from the Blacks. It was time to move on.

There was a brief hold-up, their hostess informed them all, while a helicopter took one of the passengers away.

Kelsie settled into her seat and glanced out the window as she waited to see what would transpire in the crossing. She watched a helicopter take off and wished she could get on her plane now and head back home.

She hadn't been sure what to expect of the next hour but it hadn't been coach travel and three border controls as well as immigration control, where they all needed to actually get out of the coaches, troop through the customs and immigration, and have their passports stamped.

It became less glamorous by the second as once everyone was back on board their driver navigated the maze of transit lanes and down into a train shell that encapsulated their coach for the trip under the Channel.

Kelsie felt a tiny twinge of claustrophobia as their compartment was sealed and the coach engine switched off.

The hostess had handed out bottles of cold water and then picked up the microphone. 'All lights and air will be shut down now and just letting you know it can get hot if there are delays.'

There were groans from the occupants and she hastened on. 'Usually it only takes about thirty-five minutes once we've started.'

'But we haven't started yet,' the coach driver said cheerfully. Then proceeded to share. 'We'll be in the tunnel, which is about forty metres under the Channel. Coaches and vans travel in one type of railway carrier and cars have a double-decker carrier, while lorries have carriers with open sides.' He looked up into the rear-view mirror so he could watch the faces. 'And there is an emergency tunnel running parallel to our tunnel in case of fire.'

Kelsie shuddered and decided she'd fly across if she ever came to France again.

Half an hour later, without drama of any kind, they popped out the other end into the English countryside, and she even spotted the famous white horse of Dover on the hillside as their coach zipped them towards Folkestone.

When they pulled up in the station, despite the English sleet a brass band jazzed them onto their new train and the mood, flattened by the officialdom and dimness of the tunnel, lifted again as the hostesses pointed out a printed list on the station wall that allocated their carriage by name.

Kelsie was destined for 'Audrey', and she could see the white dining cars laden with crockery as she spotted the beautiful Pullman carriage that would carry her to London—on her own. Peacefully. Without Connor Black.

Except that Winsome found her. At least there was no Connor cruising along behind her, though she couldn't help a glance back to see if he was there.

'May I join you? I'm all alone. Connor was called away.' Winsome was puffing a little and Kelsie thought she looked a little pale. 'And I haven't got your address. Or given you mine.'

There'd been a reason for that. Then the end of the sentence clicked in. She blinked. 'Called away? From the station?'

'No. From Calais. In the helicopter. One of his patients may have gone into labour.'

'Oh?' Kelsie would have taken more notice if she'd known it had been Connor soaring off. She didn't envy him the crossing in this weather. Served him right. Black widow indeed.

'Apparently his patient rang him very early this morning and after brunch, so he thought he might need to go. It wasn't too much of a shock when he abandoned me.'

He'd abandoned me, too, Kelsie thought, or maybe I abandoned him? But she didn't say it. At least he'd told his grandmother he was going, but, then, his gran had probably been nicer to him than she'd been.

Later, when she had time to think clearly, she would have to consider whether that had been a factor in him leaving her cabin so precipitously. Maybe even why he'd left? She needed to think hard about that. But Winsome was looking at her hopefully.

What was she thinking? Winsome was all alone.

'I'm sorry. You poor thing. I'd love you to join me. I was feeling quite sad that I might not see you again,' Kelsie said with a smile.

Winsome settled down opposite Kelsie in the big plush seat and they both gazed at the silver '1927' plate above the doorway.

'You haven't got rid of me yet.' It was said quietly and Kelsie wasn't even sure if she was supposed to have heard, and she chewed her lip as she tried not to laugh.

'I love these carriages,' Winsome said in a louder voice. 'The way they've created scenery in the wood. Look at that castle there. All made out of slivers of different-coloured wood.'

Kelsie pointed. 'You've got an island and palm trees above your head, there. Just under the luggage rack.' Winsome craned her neck and Kelsie hoped she didn't strain her back as the older lady bounced around in the seat to look at all the murals made of wood.

A tall, ridiculously handsome waiter in formal white tails trimmed with gold braid bowed, imparted his name as Samuel, and offered them a glass of champagne.

Surprisingly, even Winsome declined more bubbly, but nodded vigorously when he suggested tea.

Along came the silver teapots, sandwiches, caviar and quail eggs, pikelets and the inevitable scones and clotted cream. When the trolley with pastries and cakes was offered, Kelsie could see that nearly everyone shook their heads and declined. She didn't blame them.

She was learning to taste the array of food only. Neither of them had spoken for the last five minutes and Kelsie felt obliged to open conversation. 'Connor missed another lovely meal.'

The quail-egg wafer stopped halfway to Winsome's mouth and landed back down on her plate as if she'd been waiting for just such an opportunity. 'I want to talk to you about Connor. Do you mind?

Kelsie bit back a laugh. As if I could stop you, she thought, but it was a poor choice of topic, Kelsie admonished herself. 'Why should I mind?'

'How much do you know about Connor's childhood?'

Actually, he'd always been more interested in her childhood but she knew a little. 'That he lost his mother at a young age and he didn't get on well with his stepmother.'

Winsome was nodding. 'Both true. You know he was there when his mother died. Did he tell you that?'

Kelsie felt cold all over. 'No. Just that she'd drowned when he was twelve.'

Winsome looked sadly surprised. 'I thought he might have told you more. He changed from a happy-go-lucky boy to a serious young man that day.' She sighed. 'All of us changed.'

Winsome shook her head with regret. 'He told me once it was his fault. That he should have told her to come back. Shouted it out. It's funny how youngsters can blame themselves for something they have no control over.'

Winsome gazed into the distant past. 'I always blamed his father but really it was my daughter's fault. She was headstrong. Impulsive. She was always losing things. Took after me in the way she'd misplace things like her handbag, her purse, keys—it used to drive Connor's father mad but she'd just sail on serenely.

'The day she died she'd lost her engagement ring

in a rock pool, and she left Connor on the beach, even though the tide was coming in.'

Winsome sighed. 'A freak wave came, she hit her head badly, and it didn't end well.'

Kelsie remembered the serious young man who'd been the Connor she'd known. How good she'd always felt when she'd made him laugh. How good he'd said he felt when he cared for her. 'He was always going to be a doctor.'

Winsome sighed again and looked at Kelsie. 'I think he felt at some deep level it was his life's work to care for the people he loved from that day on.' She smiled softly. 'Caring for people. He has been there every inch of the way since my husband died. I was ready to curl up and die then but Connor made me sit up and believe I still had a life to live. That's not a bad trait to have.'

'So the loss of his mother is what made him so controlling.'

'Controlling?' Winsome's head came up. 'He's not controlling, not in a negative way.' She laughed. 'He cares. Worries. Gives in all the time to me, but he worries all the same, and, yes, sometimes I humour that and allow him to boss me around a little. But that's not controlling. He doesn't do it for his own gratification.'

The old lady looked concerned. 'He might have seemed that way to you,' she continued. 'You probably did need time to spread your wings before marriage and luckily you were tough enough to take it. Sometimes you just have to trust your instincts.'

She shrugged. 'And it hasn't all been bad for Connor. He loves his work. Has made a difference to so many couples. And, yes, with the work he does now, he does have to weigh risks and make decisions so he can help a woman come to a viable pregnancy, and he's used to organising things.'

The faded blue eyes looked directly at Kelsie. 'But Connor's nowhere near controlling. What on earth made you think that?'

'My father was a very domineering man. Worse when he drank. My mother left him, one Christmas, when I was fourteen. She died not long after and I never saw her again.' She looked out the window where lonely countryside stretched away into the distance. 'I vowed I would never let someone run my life again. Or ruin it.'

Winsome shook her head. 'No wonder you weren't sure you were doing the right thing, getting married, if your home was unhappy.'

Then her eyes focused on Kelsie and her voice didn't waver. 'But Connor is a world away from how you say your father was. I think it would be quite normal to have trust issues after that.'

Was that true? Was that a big part of the reason she'd run that day? She'd thought about it a lot since then. Had she been scared to love because of her parents' bad marriage? 'It's probably why I've never really been into Christmas since then, though Connor bought me a little tree once.' She thought about that and couldn't help but smile. 'It was very cute.'

Winsome studied her with sympathy. 'That's the sort of thing Connor does.' But she frowned as she thought it through. 'So you left Connor all those years ago because you thought he was like your father?'

Had she? 'I guess a few things were said when I left home that started me thinking. It seemed to fit into a few thoughts I'd already had about wishing I could just run my own life for a change. But blaming Connor doesn't seem quite as logical when I look at it now.'

Did it mean that Connor had never been the reason she'd run away? Was that how it had been? Was that why she'd still not found a man she was comfortable to share her life with? Or was it because she'd been waiting for the magic she'd experienced with Connor? She didn't want to consider that she'd blown it with him for a second time.

Winsome was gazing off into the distance. 'A good marriage is worth waiting for.'

Kelsie thought about the man Connor had become, how wonderful he'd been with Anna and her baby, his sense of humour, his sincere affection for his grandmother, the way he'd held her when she'd let him.

Then she thought about the way he'd organised her in the run-up to their wedding that had never happened. What if none of it had been his way of controlling her but all so it would be easier for her? And she'd balked and panicked unnecessarily when she'd let him down.

She thought about the last twenty-four hours, how they had been able to talk and connect when they hadn't been fighting over silly things, how he'd made her laugh.

Winsome had reached the point of her story and Kelsie came back to the present. There was new determination in his grandmother's voice. 'He needs a life partner to give him balance.'

Didn't we all? But Kelsie wasn't going there. 'I hope he finds one.' She had such a lot to think about before they arrived.

Winsome didn't look at all put out by her noncommittal answer. In fact, she looked like the mischievous older lady from Venice all those hours ago. 'Oh, I think he will.'

Connor was having a day from hell.

His flight across the Channel had been horrendous, with turbulent wind gusts and heavy sleet, and he decided he hated helicopters almost as much as trains.

Plus he'd been unsure if he had done the right thing by his grandmother or by Kelsie, but at least they'd been on the ground. Safe in the damn train.

It hadn't actually snowed on the flight but it had been falling heavily on the wild drive to the hospital.

Connie Wilson's labour was being stubborn. Stuck in the on-off contraction phase that robbed the mother of sleep. Her uterus contracted irregularly and inconsistently in strength, and therefore she wasn't any closer to actual birth but a lot closer to exhaustion. It was a pattern of an hour of contractions, none for two hours, three hours of contractions, and then none.

Connie and Harry were physically and emotionally exhausted and stressed and he felt bad that he hadn't been there earlier to allay their fears.

'Latent phase of labour is unpredictable,' he explained for the third time in a quiet voice. 'It's much more difficult to look at this slow start as a natural progression, especially when you have gone through so many medical procedures to finally get to this stage.'

He crouched down beside Connie and looked into her frightened eyes. 'It is normal, though.' He didn't say it could go on like this for days.

Connie smiled damply. 'I know. They told us in prenatal classes. And again when we arrived here this morning. But I guess I needed to hear it from you. Thank you for coming. I do appreciate it.'

She shrugged. 'Maybe I don't have the faith in my body that I should have but it has let me down. We couldn't fall pregnant without help and I just worry I won't be able to give birth to our baby without help.'

He understood that. Wished he could do more. 'That's perfectly understandable but I believe in your body's ability to do this. And you can take comfort that it's a very common mindset from parents who have gone through assisted reproduction, like you have.'

She sighed. 'And you have kept telling me I'm not sick or a patient.'

Connor looked at the worried father. 'That's because everything is normal. The baby's monitoring has shown lots of reserves yet, but as her mum you need a good sleep.'

At least Connie was listening but he could feel the tension vibrating from Harry and he'd bet Kelsie would say it wasn't helping Connie's body to relax when they all knew her husband was desperately impatient to see their baby and his wife safely at the end of this pregnancy from hell.

'Exactly!' Harry pounced on the opportunity to have input. 'She needs sleep. So let's do something about it. Can't we finish this business with a Caesarean?' Connor could see the anxiety he was feeling because of the cumulative stresses of many miscarriages—and here they were so close to having all their dreams come true.

And he was probably on the defensive for his wife

whom he couldn't help, either physically by taking her pains or with his usual mental ability to solve problems. For a man used to running his multinational business and dealing with problems immediately, he looked like he was having a hard time being utterly powerless for once.

Connor could sympathise but he wasn't going to rush into a Caesarean just because Connie had prolonged early labour. This was his business and it was his job to make unemotional, yet correct decisions.

He didn't believe in unnecessary Caesareans because there were risks in every operation and these pregnancies were so hard to come by that statistically he dealt in choosing the lesser risk. Normal birth was much less risky for mother and baby.

Connor ran his hands through his hair, unsure how to help until unexpectedly the image of Kelsie, serene and confident, on the train came to him. He looked up and caught both the worried parents' attention with his sudden smile.

Maybe it was time for a little midwifery magic. He just wished she was there to do it for him but he'd try his best.

'I believe Connie can and will do this by herself. When your baby is ready. You're doing amazingly well.' Connor recited Kelsie's words and the calm and positive way she'd said them. 'Both of you. Your baby is very determined, just like her dad and mum, but we have to wait for the labour to establish itself properly.' He pulled up a chair and sat down.

'Let me tell you a great story about what happened on the way over in the train.'

Connie's eyes grew wider as Connor explained about Anna's baby's decision to arrive between countries, in a train and feet first, and as he concluded his tale with how he'd seen them that morning before Paris and how well they'd both looked, Connie sighed back into the bed. He saw her search out her husband's eyes and nod.

'Maybe I could have one of those sleeping tablets we keep refusing and just have a rest. Wait for it to happen instead of being so determined it has to happen this minute. I do want a birth like that.'

Connor stood up. 'I want you to have a birth like that too.'

He smiled, could feel the tension dissipate in the room as they finally accepted a delay in their expectations. 'I can't promise you a train carriage but I can promise you a couple of hours' sleep.

'The good news is that a large percentage of women do wake up in labour after a sedation at this point. So hopefully you'll be one of them.'

He looked at Harry. 'They have a desk you can use for work if you don't want to leave the building, but I do think you should leave Connie to rest when she gets the sedation. She could text you when she wakes up.'

Harry looked at his wife. 'Is that okay with you, Con?'

She nodded. 'I am very tired.'

'Let's get this sorted, then.' Connor glanced at his watch. The train wasn't due into Victoria for another two hours.

If Connie went into labour he'd have to arrange for someone else to meet Winsome. He'd set that up just in case. In the back of his mind he still had all his balls in

the air. He knew where Kelsie was heading tonight and
he still had time to talk to her before she left.

Back in the Pullman carriages, rattling towards London, Kelsie and Winsome had passed the towers and
keeps of the English countryside during the meal, leaving behind the manors and ploughed paddocks of the
country towns.

Passengers were dozing in their seats, replete or even
having over-indulged, and the waiters had begun clear-
ing the tables as they began to pass through more sub-
urban areas.

Soon they would arrive at Victoria and Winsome had
settled back in her seat with her eyes closed.

Kelsie was wondering if Connor had arrived in time
to be there for his client's birth. She knew how scared
fertility-challenged parents could become. She'd had a
recent client of her own who'd had IVF and had been
an absolute mess prior to labour.

Shelby had had so many pre-conception visits, so
much intense screening and medication to achieve conception, and then such a tense time dreading a miscar-
riage until the first three months had passed, that when
her IVF clinic had sent her back to her old hospital as
a now low-risk patient, she hadn't been used to being
left to progress naturally.

Kelsie had coached Shelby and her husband in the
prenatal classes, a weekend course, and the improve-
ment in Shelby's self-confidence and positive birth out-
look had been miraculous. She wondered if they had
such classes in the UK and suddenly it was something
she wanted to talk to Connor about.

Anyway, she didn't need to go there. She'd be flying back to Australia very soon. Shelby and her husband had had a gorgeous birth not long before Kelsie had come away. When she got home she looked forward to visiting that little family.

Home. Her comfy flat. Her friends. It was ridiculous to think she wouldn't settle back into it all easily just because she'd met up with an old boyfriend. One who might even be keen for her to stay around.

Who was she kidding? Not just met.

Slept with.

Actually, they hadn't slept. They'd made incredible, amazing, mind-blowing love. She'd glimpsed a world she hadn't really believed existed before.

Seen that Connor held a part of her that nobody else would ever touch. And then they'd bickered their way back to being strangers. How had that happened?

You couldn't just forget that sort of encounter. But that was what she'd have to do or risk driving herself mad.

She looked across at Connor's grandmother, and noticed Winsome rub her chest and frown as her eyes flicked open. In fact, she did look a little pale and not at all happy.

'Are you all right?' Kelsie asked softly.

'I might just have a wee nap. Wake me when we get there.'

Kelsie narrowed her eyes and studied Winsome as she closed her eyes. The older lady's cheeks were white and the tiny frown on her forehead made the soft wrinkles there pucker more than usual.

'Are you in pain?' Kelsie didn't know whether to bother her or not.

Pale blue eyes fluttered open again, accompanied by a rueful smile as she rubbed her chest. 'I'm a bit sore in the chest. Probably from overeating but it's starting to bother me. I thought a wee nap might help.'

'Have you had it before?' Kelsie stood up and leaned over the older lady's chair. 'Let me check your pulse.' She took Winsome's wrist in her fingers and felt for the pulse under the soft skin. There it was. Bounding along a little faster than she would have expected.

'Sometimes I get reflux.' She glanced around at the quiet carriage and grimaced with embarrassment.

Kelsie regarded her shrewdly. 'And does this feel like that?'

Winsome began to look extremely miserable. 'It's getting worse.' Big eyes looked mournfully at Kelsie. 'My husband died of a sudden heart attack, you know. I can't help thinking of that, even though I'm sure it's not anything like that. I just wish Connor hadn't left.'

Kelsie squeezed Winsome's hand. 'We're almost at Victoria and we'll get you to a doctor.'

Winsome bit her lip to stop the quiver. 'I want Connor.'

Kelsie's heart squeezed. 'I know. You'll be fine. I'll stay with you until we find him again.'

One large tear rolled down Winsome's cheek and Kelsie clasped her hand. 'I'll find Connor for you.'

She pushed the service button and while she waited she thought about the food and alcohol offered over the last thirty-six hours and how Winsome had been magnificent in her capacity.

It could just be gastrooesophageal reflux. Her skin chilled. Or it could be cardiac chest pain. She didn't want to think that but she needed to get someone to see Winsome before Connor's grandmother did something Kelsie couldn't handle by herself.

Where was Connor when they needed him? She'd be very happy for him to take control now. He should not have left his grandmother alone. And she'd tell him so. For some strange reason she felt calmer after that decision, and not just because it meant she would see him at least one more time.

She looked back at her patient. 'If you were ever going to get indigestion, I imagine this would be a popular time.' She glanced around the cabin and saw most of the patrons had their eyes shut. 'What do you usually take when you get that?'

'My antacid tablets. I forgot to take the prescription one this morning. But they're in the luggage compartment.' She glanced around as if searching. 'I wish Connor was here.'

Kelsie nodded. She did too, and moved back to her seat and reached up to the ornate silver luggage rack and pulled down her tote. In her bag she had some lozenges so she dug around until she found them.

'How about you take one of my little over-the-counter antacid tablets?' She glanced into her bag again. 'And two of my travel aspirins, which would be about half a normal dose of aspirin. That will cover both bases while we wait for help.' Aspirin was always a good first-aid suggestion with cardiac pain or clots. They had done a lot of sitting and maybe Winsome was in more danger than she thought.

Samuel, the steward, appeared at her elbow and Kelsie turned to him with relief. 'Mrs Black has chest pain. How long until we arrive in London?'

Samuel looked instantly concerned and frowned over Winsome's increasing pallor. He spoke quietly, for Kelsie's hearing only. 'About ten minutes. I can arrange for an ambulance to meet us, if you wish?'

Kelsie nodded just as Winsome whimpered and rubbed her chest again. 'Do you feel breathless?'

'Just with the pain.' She sounded more frail than Kelsie expected and her concern climbed. 'It's difficult to breathe deeply. I just want Connor.' Her voice faded away and she closed her eyes.

Kelsie's heart settled a little at that. Cardiac chest pain shouldn't get worse with inhalation, which made it more likely to be another cause. But it still needed checking. She looked at Samuel then back at Winsome. 'We'll have that ambulance, thanks.'

It seemed to take for ever for the train to pull into the station.

The loudspeaker boomed as they came to a stop. 'Would all passengers please remain seated for the first five minutes while we transfer an ill passenger off the train. Your luggage will be waiting for you once they have been transferred. Thank you.'

Kelsie followed the ambulance officers, who had fireman-lifted Winsome out of the carriage onto the bench seat of another small luggage train, and Kelsie followed onto the platform and the organised chaos of Victoria Station. A row of luggage trolleys laden with Christmas goodies from Europe had arrived and the porters were lining bags up in neat rows for identification and retrieval.

Kelsie saw her suitcase, which towered over the others, almost waving at her, and she grimaced at that problem for later. Winsome first.

They trundled through to a side entrance, where an ambulance waited.

She glanced back into the crowded station. Could she accompany Winsome?

She knew she wanted to but a glance inside the small emergency vehicle didn't seem to suggest a lot of room and she doubted they'd let her. That was when she realised the snow was melting on her hair and face. Landing quite heavily on her and the snaking line of people at the cab rank.

It would be hell to catch a cab in this on Christmas Eve but she'd feel she'd let Winsome down if she abandoned her to strangers.

A young woman appeared at her elbow. 'I'm to meet Mrs Winsome Black. Was that who was just lifted into that ambulance?'

The young woman was dressed from head to foot in black suede, very chic, but Kelsie decided she looked almost like a seal. Even the scarf threaded around her neck was suede to match the cap she wore over her hair.

But seal or not, Kelsie pounced on her with relief. 'Yes. She has chest pain. Do you have contact with Dr Black?'

The girl's eyes widened in distress. 'I can get a message to him.' The girl scrolled through her contact list. 'I've already arranged with a porter to have her luggage collected.' The young woman looked up enquiringly. 'And you are?'

Kelsie blinked, calmed a little now that Winsome was in good hands, and replayed the girl's words in her head. Well, who was she?

She glanced once into the ambulance but Winsome was being assessed by paramedics and perhaps she wasn't needed now. She turned away. She almost said, 'No one important,' but before the words were out she was stopped by a familiar, if frail voice.

'She's with me.' Winsome's voice drifted from the rear of the ambulance and Kelsie had to turn and smile. It seemed Winsome Black didn't miss anything—even when miserably unwell in the back of an ambulance.

Well, then. She'd better stay. 'I'm Mrs Black's companion until she's seen by Dr Black.' It was actually a huge relief because she would have worried all night that Connor hadn't managed to find his grandmother and that Winsome hadn't recovered with medical care.

'Please tell him that Kelsie has gone with her.' She saw the interest in the girl's eyes and ignored it. She'd suddenly seen a solution to another problem. 'There is a very large purple suitcase with a K. Summers nametag. Can you arrange for that to be collected, too, please? If possible, have it transferred to the Ritz. I'm booking in there later.'

The girl didn't seem fazed by the request and Kelsie supposed that Connor would hire efficient personnel. At least she wouldn't have to wrestle with her bag and if she lost it then it wasn't a life-or-death matter. Possibly unlike Winsome—until she could be sure.

She'd phone the hotel from the hospital when she knew Winsome was okay.

The paramedic tapped her on the shoulder. 'Excuse me, miss. Would you please reassure Mrs Black that you're coming with us? She won't let us shut the doors. You can travel with the driver.'

Kelsie's distraction evaporated. The most important person here was Winsome. 'Of course.' When she peered in past the folded doors her new friend's eyes were huge with fear and she leant in and clasped her hand. 'I'm here. I'll be in the front and I'll find Connor.'

'Tell them to take me to St Douglas's Private Hospital.'

Kelsie looked at the men. 'Can you do that?' It wouldn't work like that in Australia.

The paramedic nodded. 'The main hospitals are very busy and it would be quicker than through their emergency department anyway.'

CHAPTER THIRTEEN

AT THE SAME time, to Connor's relief, Connie Wilson woke up in strong labour and as far as her pregnancy went, the waiting was almost over. Thanks to all the stop-start contractions her labour progressed rapidly through first stage, and if he didn't get to meet the train he couldn't complain because he would meet the new baby Wilson and be there for her parents.

The room was quiet, peaceful, and Connor stood, apparently relaxed, at the end of the bed, waiting. It was always the same and the tension never left him until the baby was safe in its mother's arms but neither his patients nor staff ever guessed that.

'I love you,' Connor heard Harry Wilson whisper to his wife, raw emotion thick in his voice, and for one fractured second Connor felt a sudden surge of loss so great he actually flinched. Why didn't he have the chance to share this moment with the woman he had always loved?

But he pulled his thoughts back to the moment. He'd tried and failed and unless he did something soon, she'd be gone from his life once again.

When he glanced back at Harry the man's eyes were suspiciously bright as they darted nervously to Connor and then back at his wife. But Connie was elsewhere, concentrating in her own world, as she strained to ease her baby down the birth canal.

There was a little while to go but the end was drawing closer and then everyone could relax.

A senior midwife appeared around the curtain and crossed to whisper in Connor's ear. 'You have a phone call at the desk.'

If it had been anyone less unflappable he would have glared a refusal but the midwife in charge was no fool. So what could be this important? 'Can you tell them I'll ring back?'

'It's about your grandmother. Apparently she's been admitted downstairs with chest pain.'

He closed his eyes. Looked back at Harry and Connie. Estimated the amount of time he had before the birth. There was no sign of the baby yet, Connie had just started pushing, but would it upset them if he left, even for a few minutes? The last thing he wanted was to stress Connie. But what if his gran was critically ill?

His grandmother had always been there for him and it was his responsibility to ensure she had the best care. It was his responsibility that everyone had the best care.

Unexpectedly Connie leaned up on her elbow and panted at him. Waved him away with her hand. 'For goodness' sake. Go and see if your gran is okay. We'll be here when you come back.' Connie waved him away again. 'Go. Hurry. I'm busy.' And went back to pushing.

He stared at Connie in astonishment, shook his head with a smile and went. Swiftly. There was a junior midwife standing at the lift, holding it for him, and he shot her a warm thank-you glance, then looked back over his shoulder at the senior midwife. She shooed him off, too. 'I'll page you when we get close.'

When the lift doors opened on the ground floor the first person he saw was Kelsie. His relief was enormous. He hadn't lost her yet. And she'd been with his gran in her time of need.

He allowed himself one brief, soul-enriching look and then scanned ahead. 'Where is she?'

'She's being assessed by the physician. She's okay, Connor. She was in a lot of pain but I think it's reflux, though they're ruling out cardiac or a clot. She demanded they bring her here.'

'She's a fighter,' he reassured himself more than Kelsie. Then glanced back at the lift. Kelsie had said hs grandmother was okay. Did he believe Kelsie? He should go back to the Wilsons. But he couldn't. 'I want to see her.'

'Of course you do. She wants to see you too.' Kelsie led the way. Knocked on a door and opened it on a room where a tall gangly man in a black suit stood beside the bed. Winsome looked pale, and very still, with her eyes closed.

'Ah. Connor.' The man put out his hand and Connor shook it briefly. 'I've given her something for the pain and she's a bit drowsy now. We're about to run an ECG to check her heart, and then we'll scan her, but I hear she's been on that train, living the high life again.'

'My fault. I went with her this time.' He stepped closer to the bed. Picked up his grandmother's hand and squeezed it between both of his. Her eyelids fluttered and she smiled drowsily up at him.

He pretended to frown at her. 'You said you'd managed for eighty years without me.'

'I'll be fine. Soon.' Her eyes closed again.

She looked so pale, he thought. 'What about her bloods?'

'We're waiting for results. But she's tough. Given herself a scare, though.'

His heart squeezed with the dilemma of staying or leaving to go back upstairs. 'She's given me one as well.'

'She'll be fine with rest. I'll keep her in overnight.' The doctor's pager bleeped and he excused himself. Connor took a step to pick up the clinical notes when his own name was paged over the loudspeaker.

'Would Dr Black please go to Maternity immediately.'

He glanced up at the speaker. Torn. 'It's Connie's baby.'

Kelsie watched his indecision with a surge of empathy. Poor Connor. The struggle. He wanted to do everything. This was the Connor she knew. Bless him. All of it was good. 'You can't do everyone's jobs. Or save everyone. You go and do yours. I'll stay here until you get back.'

'She's the closest thing I've had to a mother for so many years. I love her. I don't want to let her down.'

Kelsie understood that. She understood a lot of things now. 'You couldn't let her down. Your grandmother is in good hands. The doctor is great. Go. I'll be here.'

He nodded. He trusted Kelsie to stay with her until he could return.

'You're right.' Unexpectedly, he paused and searched

her face, said, 'I would have been there for you, you know,' before he dropped a swift kiss on her lips and spun away.

She heard his voice again as he disappeared. 'Hold that lift.'

Kelsie touched her lips with her fingers. He would have been where for her? She could still feel the imprint of Connor's mouth on hers.

She didn't understand his comment but wished she'd kissed him back, one last time, then hugged the feeling that he had trusted her with the most important person in his life. Anything else was too complicated to think about.

An hour later Connor was back. 'Baby Wilson has arrived!' There was immense satisfaction as well as quiet relief in his voice and Kelsie smiled.

'A bouncing baby girl who's taken to the outside world with a calm acceptance that's left her besotted parents very happy.'

She loved it that he glowed with relief. He was a very good man. 'I'm so glad you were there for them.'

He grinned at her. Almost buckled her knees with the power of it. 'Me too. Thank you for staying here so I didn't have to worry about Gran.'

'My pleasure.' She'd been glad she could help him but it was over now. Everything was over and she should go. They didn't need her any more. 'Dr Miles has been back. Your grandmother's tests have all come back negative, as well as the positive result from the medication treating her reflux. So it all points to that being the cause.'

She pinned a bright smile on her face, even though she was suddenly feeling very flat for no reason at all. Which should have been bizarre with this handsome man smiling at her like she was the embodiment of Christmas. 'So everything has turned out well.'

Except now she needed to leave. 'And I have to get to my hotel. Now that you're back. Check my bag made it.'

His smile dimmed. 'I'll take you.'

She smiled, realising she couldn't help the swift lift in her spirits and that in itself frightened her. Very much. No. It was better to make the break now. Stop dragging out this painful feeling of loss. Leave Connor with his gran in private.

Though the reasoning was hard to pin down right at this second as she looked at Connor. She wanted to hug him and share his relief that his gran would be fine. All she knew was that this goodbye hurt. 'Don't worry about it. I can catch a cab.'

The humour had faded from his face. 'I said I'll take you.'

He couldn't leave the hospital and they both knew it. 'What about your grandmother?'

'Max will be here in a minute. We'll go as soon as he arrives. She'll sleep for a couple of hours yet and Max will stay with her.'

She shook her head. 'I'll catch a cab.'

'Not on Christmas Eve you can't.' Connor could feel his frustration building. Why couldn't she at least let him do this for her?

Would this roller-coaster day never end? So much had happened and he didn't want her to leave until they'd had a chance to talk.

She was backing away towards the door and he followed her. Glanced once over his shoulder at his sleeping grandmother and decided this was better dealt with outside in the corridor than in a sick room.

'Goodbye, Connor. Give my love to your grandmother when she wakes up.'

What was she doing? Had he got it so badly wrong? Didn't the way they'd made love mean anything to her?

He suspected it had and they needed to talk about it. It shouldn't be rushed but she'd be out of here in seconds. Like she was afraid of him.

Connor fought to hang onto his feeling of impending doom. He wanted to ask her to stay. Give what they had a chance. But she was going. Leaning towards the exit as she waited for him to return her goodbye.

Tomorrow she'd be gone from the country. And he hadn't had enough time to know if they were right together or still so very, very wrong.

Though even in the brief time since they'd parted he had more faith in his own feelings for her than he had in Kelsie's for him—and damn right he was scared that she'd leave him at the last minute if he opened himself up to loving her again. What if he never recovered?

He ran his hands through his hair. She was the only woman, apart from his mother, whom he should have told to come back, who'd torn his heart. Should he risk it all yet again, and ask her to stay?

He glanced up and down the deserted corridor but nobody was in sight.

For a moment he wished he'd never got on that damn train and met her again. 'Stop, Kelsie.'

She paused, turned back to him.

It was now or never and he couldn't bear the thought of never. 'I gave you my heart once before and you walked away from me. Unlike my mother, you didn't give me the chance to say come back, so I'm doing it now. I want you to stay.' But he was terrified he was going to lose at the last minute again.

It hadn't been the most romantic declaration. He couldn't believe what this woman did to him. How insane this entire crazy day had been. How desperate he suddenly felt. He couldn't believe he'd mentioned his mother. His loss. That he'd admitted he would be the one hurt if it didn't work out—so much for not putting himself out there again.

She shook her head. 'I can't. We're the same as we always were. On different sides of the world. But it was wonderful seeing you, Connor. Goodbye.'

So she'd missed the whole point. Though he had to admit it wasn't surprising seeing as his declaration had been so garbled. But he didn't believe distance would keep them apart.

Kelsie had no idea what she was saying. She was desperate to get away before she burst into tears. Her brain was all fogged again with the emotion this guy could stir up in her. Not all of it was good emotion because if she admitted she was wrong now then maybe she'd been wrong fifteen years ago and she'd been responsible for all that wasted time. It didn't bear thinking about. Not at this moment anyway.

She watched him run his hand through his hair. He did that a lot when he was stressed. And she had caused him this stress and she was sorry for that.

He was saying, 'Please. Let me take you to your hotel

and we can talk. You said you're not leaving until to-morrow. And you don't even have to go then. Stay and have a drink with me.'

Almost with relief she seized on the argument her brain would listen to. Nothing had changed with him. This was why she'd run away from him before. He didn't listen when she said she needed her own space.

She took a couple of deep breaths. His face was se-rious. Determined, yet there was a vulnerability about him she hadn't seen before. It was that that made her pause. They began to walk towards the lifts together, even though she hadn't agreed.

Then he spoiled it. 'Do you really have to fly back to Australia tomorrow?'

Her voice quieted as a nurse approached. 'I have to. I have a ticket. And I start work in seven days. My pa-tients need me.'

He frowned. Shook his head. 'Can't you delay your flights?' He pushed the lift call button with unneces-sary force. 'Put them off!'

'Why?'

'I'm asking you to stay.'

'I *can't*.' Couldn't he understand she'd organised her life too?

'We need more time.'

And there it was again. *Give in, Kelsie. Do what I want.* She'd fought damn hard for her independence. Paid a huge price for it too, including the loss of the man in front of her. Had worked hard for respect in her profession. For the trust of the women she cared for. She'd like to see him fly away from his patients for her. He obviously didn't care about the women she'd looked after during their whole pregnancies. 'No, Connor. I won't do that.'

'I see.' No expression. How did he do that?

She wanted to stamp her feet and scream at him.

He stopped and in that same expressionless voice, 'Then I'm sorry I pushed you to stay.'

'Have a good Christmas, Connor. Give my love to your grandmother. I'll get my own cab.'

He sighed heavily and turned away and she couldn't help but wonder if her damned independence was worth the loss of this man—again.

Connor woke on Christmas morning and he'd never felt so alone. With sudden clarity he knew he didn't want to wake and feel like this ever again.

It wasn't too late. She hadn't flown home yet. He just needed a chance to tell her he would come to her in Australia as soon as he could.

He hadn't really expected her to cancel her flights. They'd discussed that, he thought with a wry smile. When he'd panicked and pressured her to suspend all her flights and plans just because he'd said they should spend more time together. He couldn't say he blamed her for storming off.

But he wanted to explain more eloquently that he was now certain they were meant for each other. If he could just see her one more time he would let her know he'd wait for her.

That he'd fight for her.

To hell with it. He knew he was strong enough, determined enough to take that chance again or even as many times as it took. That risking everything for Kelsie's love would always be worth it—but he needed to stop rushing her. Let her come to that decision in her own way, in her own time.

Max had pulled some Orient Express Christmas Eve strings at his request and filled his special order so Kelsie would get his Christmas surprise before she left for the airport. There was a slim chance he'd have already missed her by the time he'd arranged his grandmother's discharge but he could deal with that.

Because once Gran was sorted he doubted he'd have much to do, and he could be on the next plane out to Australia, judging by the way Max had taken charge of Winsome since he'd arrived at the hospital last evening.

If he had missed her then, considering he and Kelsie had waited fifteen years to meet again, he could wait a few days more until he could arrange a flight. But he didn't want to wait.

Christmas Day and Kelsie woke to a blanket of snow outside the Ritz's windows. Her first white Christmas. In a famous and luxurious hotel in a city she'd always wanted to visit. So why was her mood so black?

Ahh. She put her hand over her eyes. Not that word. Black.

Connor Black. It was too late now but she should have had that drink last night. Should have taken the chance that Connor was right. She missed him this morning.

Maybe there was still time to catch him before she flew out.

She scrabbled in her bag for the number of the hospital the nurse had given her and she dialled shakily.

The doctor had said Winsome would be able to go home early Christmas morning. But when she phoned the hospital they'd already left. Connor had picked her up already. The only good thing was that Winsome was now much more comfortable on the correct medication. Thank goodness it hadn't been her heart that was the trouble.

Kelsie wished she could say the same for her own heart. But she too would recover with the right treatment. Namely a flight as far away from London as possible and a whole lot of work, but first she had to get through the morning.

There was a knock at the door and she put the phone down as she glanced at the clock.

It was the arrival of breakfast, and when it was pushed in, it looked like a Christmas feast in miniature. A tiny, holly-decorated painted bowl of muesli, strawberries, honey yoghurt and steaming Earl Grey tea.

Under the silver dome was a tiny nativity scene, complete with dozing animals, surrounded by curls of bacon and egg and French toast. It looked so cute she had to smile. Albeit a watery one. On the tray was a tiny, exquisitely wrapped box with a card and she smiled again as the waiter backed away.

He seemed to be waiting for her to open the card so she slid her finger under the seal and lifted the stiff folded paper out. She expected it to be from the hotel to go with the little unopened present.

Santa has been. There's something outside the door. Merry Christmas, Kelsie!

She looked up and as if he'd been waiting for her to read it the waiter stopped at the door.

'Someone has left you something outside your door, madam. Would you like me to bring it in?'

'Yes, please.'

It was a tiny carry-on suitcase, in gold, with a ribbon around it. She frowned as she circled it and then lifted it onto the bed to open. Inside lay a gorgeous little Christmas tree, sprinkled with gold and covered in tiny fibreoptic lights.

It looked suspiciously like the one from the Orient Express dining car. She guessed the suitcase was so she could fly it home. Why did that thought make her eyes sting and her throat close?

Was Connor here? Her heart leapt and she looked quickly up at the waiter. 'And the gentleman?'

The man shook his head mournfully. Obviously he was a romantic. 'There is no gentleman.'

She crossed to the dresser and plugged the little tree in and watched it turn as the man left, quietly closing the door behind him. The tree spun and sparkled and shimmered like it had in the dining car where she and Connor had eaten together last night.

Tears stung her eyes but she blinked them away. Surely she'd done the right thing. And it was too late now anyway.

She turned back to the wrapped box on her breakfast tray and slowly unwrapped the stiff paper from the gift. Inside lay the silver charm bracelet from the Orient Express, complete with a tiny porter's hat like Wolfgang's, a miniature guard's whistle, a little train engine and a teddy bear.

There was a note.

*I'm not asking you to stay. I'm asking if I can
come and visit you in Australia as soon as I can
arrange a flight.*

'I think that would be wonderful,' she whispered to
the empty room.

He was so much better at this than she was. She
glanced at the phone again. One more try and she at
least had the house number that Winsome had given her.

But that phone just rang unanswered too.

Time was running out and the airport waited. Maybe
he would follow her to Australia, as he'd said. She could
only hope so.

It took Kelsie two hours to get to the airport through
the snow and as the cab driver dropped her off the radio
cheerfully informed them that flights had a two-hour
delay due to the snow. Too long to wait. Too short to
jump back into the cab and search for Connor.

'What you want to do, lady?'

She thought about the suitcase. 'Just drop me. I'll
stay here until my flight opens.'

'You sure?'

'Yep.' She saw his shoulders lift and he pulled the
car into the drop-off point. She paid him and the rat
didn't get out of the car, just popped the boot so she'd
have to lift her huge case out herself. Connor would
never do that to her.

'Merry Christmas,' she said with her most winning
smile, and he had the grace to look away. As she got

out she heard his door open and he grumbled his way to the rear of the vehicle and heaved her bag onto the pavement for her.

'Good luck with getting that on the plane,' he said. Then he grinned, shook his head and wished her luck before he drove away.

Kelsie encouraged the wheels on her suitcase to ignore the snow, but they weren't listening so she tipped it on its side and dragged it, and her new little gold suitcase along with it, while the icy wind bit into her cheeks. It wasn't the only part of her that was cold.

Home would be humid. Christmas week would be sunshine and a hot wind. Sunburnt kids and ice-cream cake. Home would be great. But despite the promise of heat the words were only empty words as the wind continued to bite into her. Deeply. She'd blown it. Been a coward. But Connor had said he would come after her.

Inside the departure hall was chaotic. With the flight delays every available waiting space in the airport seemed to be filled with bodies and luggage.

And suddenly she knew. She didn't want to go. Didn't want to leave without seeing Connor one more time and telling him she loved him. He'd said he'd come to Australia but what if he never came? What if something happened to his grandmother and he couldn't come?

It was her own fault. She'd been a quitter. Waking up to Connor's gifts should have been the moment she grasped, not run away from. Should have jumped in a cab to him then and there.

And now it was too late. Her pride and her stupid independence had ruined it for her again. She turned around and dragged her suitcase towards the door but even that was difficult to traverse.

Then Kelsie saw Connor arrive and blinked. Or perhaps it was just someone she thought looked like him because she wanted him so badly.

No. It *was* him and she could feel a smile stretch right across her face. He must have been to her hotel. And the joy that had flooded her made no bones about the truth. She loved him. How could she have been so blind? It was as though for the very first time she could see who he really was. How wrong she'd been. Twice. She didn't deserve his love but she wanted it. All of it. She dragged her suitcases across the floor.

She should have known that loving Connor wouldn't take away her independence, it would bring out the best of herself. She'd so looked forward to travelling on the Orient Express, but it seemed learning to love Connor had been her true journey. If only he'd have her.

And here he was so it looked like he would have her. The man was tenacious. Even now he was giving her another chance when she'd been so determined to climb on her high horse and fly off into the sunset. Fool. But she was such a lucky fool.

She watched him cross the floor to her left. Striding tall and straight and commanding. Connor, here, opening himself up to the risk of being knocked down again. She shook her head in wonder. He'd already been let down by her so badly once before and she didn't think she could ever be that brave.

Or maybe she could?

She saw him hesitate, glance around at the sea of faces, and then he straightened and that determined look she remembered from old crossed his face. His eyes began to systematically scan the crowds. Looking for her. She dropped the handles of her bags and stepped forward towards him.

Connor felt a tap on his shoulder. 'Excuse me. Would you like my seat, sir?'

He spun around and she was smiling at him. Sky-blue eyes. Snub nose. That mouth. Here in the milling crowds, looking up at him like she'd known he would come.

Then she said something amazing. Something he'd waited fifteen years to hear. 'It's not a seat I want to give you.' She stepped into his arms. 'It's my heart. If you'll have it.'

And there was love light shining from her beautiful eyes. For him. He couldn't believe it. But he couldn't mistake it. She was lifting her face to his, waiting for his kiss. 'Merry Christmas, Connor.'

He gently touched his lips to hers. 'Merry Christmas, my love.' And he lifted her off the floor and spun her in his arms. 'I love you, you know. Always have. Always will.'

'I'm sorry, Connor. It was me who had the issues. I was scared of falling in love. Scared of losing my independence when I'd only just seen the possibilities. I put that on you. You never deserved it and I'm sorry.'

So many things made sense now. Even, perhaps, the man he was now. The way he'd organised everything when they had been younger. How he'd tried to think of everything. Kept her safe because he couldn't bear to lose her.

Connor looked down at her. Wonder and joy were

bubbling inside him. 'We were both young. And I did organise you a lot. And when that blew up in my face I thought I could control my emotions and it wouldn't happen again. Until I saw you again and you had me back on the ropes.'

'You are the bravest man I know to take me on.'

He grinned. 'Not as brave as Max. For taking on Gran.'

She had to laugh at that. Then had a thought. 'You don't live with your gran, do you?'

'No. No way. I love her dearly but we'd kill each other.' He smiled. 'I have a flat near Tower Bridge. Scared, were you?'

'No. Just wondering if we had to live in England all year round. The weather is very different from what I'm used to.'

'I'm sure I can think of ways to keep you warm. And Max and my grandmother will sort out their own lives.' He smiled at her. 'And *together*—' he stressed the word '—we'll decide the rest.'

She liked the sound of that. A lot. She remembered her presents and the little Christmas tree. Leaned up and kissed him. He tasted wonderful so she did it again.

He tilted his head. 'Hmm. What was that for? Not that I'm complaining.'

She lifted the sleeve of her coat and jiggled her wrist at him. The little Orient Express bracelet tinkled and caught the light. 'My gifts. They're beautiful. Thank you.' She looked at this tall and commanding man who had fought so hard for her. Had cared so much. 'I've only got me to offer you.'

'You are all I ever wanted for Christmas.' He leaned

in and their lips met and Kelsie softened and sighed into this gorgeous man she was not going to waste another minute not loving.

'Merry Christmas, my love.'

He squeezed her in his arms and she felt surrounded by his love. It felt so right. He whispered in her hair, 'Welcome home.'

EPILOGUE

IT WAS CHRISTMAS night one year later and Connor gently wiped the bead of sweat off Kelsie's brow as she breathed out slowly and surely.

No strenuous grunting or breath-holding, just slow breath after slow breath in the right direction, and already he could see that soon their longed-for child would arrive. He glanced at the clock. Five minutes to twelve. He smiled to himself. Kelsie had said she'd thought their baby would wait until it could have a birthday of its own and it looked like she had been right. It was obviously an independent little munchkin like its mother.

'I love you so much,' he whispered, and Kelsie's semi-focused gaze settled briefly and softly on his face before she closed her eyes again.

'Me, too,' she whispered back. There was no strain in her voice, just calm knowledge that all would happen as it should.

He'd watched her work with his nervous mothers over the last six months since they'd returned from Australia. They'd waited until all her women had birthed and then she'd been as eager as him to come back to live in England to spend time with Winsome and her new husband, Max, and prepare their own home overlooking the Thames for their new baby's arrival.

He'd eased back from his research and spent more time working together with Kelsie in his fertility clinic, here at Saint Douglas's, meeting the gap for clients who had been successful in conception but were terrified about their pregnancies and labours, and his new mothers had blossomed.

The beautiful births he'd been privileged to watch over had taken on a serene quality he'd never seen before, and the other midwives were absorbing what Kelsie had to teach them. It was like the two of them had been destined to heal childless couples—just as they had been destined to heal each other—and the joy that brought made each day a blessing.

But this was his and Kelsie's birth, their own magic, and the wonder of the moment was upon them. He squeezed his wife's hand, glanced at the clock and smiled again as his daughter arrived gently into the world.

One minute after midnight, and baby Winsome Kelsie Black opened her eyes and blinked up at her father, her mother and the brand-new world. Accidentally her little arm lifted and she waved.

Kelsie laughed. Caught his eye and blew him a kiss. Whispered, 'I love you.'

And he whispered back, 'I love you, too.' He looked down at his family. His gorgeous wife, his gorgeous daughter, and the way his arm lay across them both.

He'd buy his daughter a present. And he knew the perfect thing. A train!

* * * * *

Mills & Boon® Hardback
December 2013

ROMANCE

Defiant in the Desert	Sharon Kendrick
Not Just the Boss's Plaything	Caitlin Crews
Rumours on the Red Carpet	Carole Mortimer
The Change in Di Navarra's Plan	Lynn Raye Harris
The Prince She Never Knew	Kate Hewitt
His Ultimate Prize	Maya Blake
More than a Convenient Marriage?	Dani Collins
A Hunger for the Forbidden	Maisey Yates
The Reunion Lie	Lucy King
The Most Expensive Night of Her Life	Amy Andrews
Second Chance with Her Soldier	Barbara Hannay
Snowed in with the Billionaire	Caroline Anderson
Christmas at the Castle	Marion Lennox
Snowflakes and Silver Linings	Cara Colter
Beware of the Boss	Leah Ashton
Too Much of a Good Thing?	Joss Wood
After the Christmas Party...	Janice Lynn
Date with a Surgeon Prince	Meredith Webber

MEDICAL

From Venice with Love	Alison Roberts
Christmas with Her Ex	Fiona McArthur
Her Mistletoe Wish	Lucy Clark
Once Upon a Christmas Night...	Annie Claydon

1113 GEN STD HB

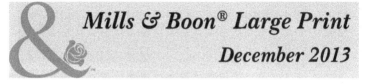

Mills & Boon® Large Print

December 2013

ROMANCE

The Billionaire's Trophy	Lynne Graham
Prince of Secrets	Lucy Monroe
A Royal Without Rules	Caitlin Crews
A Deal with Di Capua	Cathy Williams
Imprisoned by a Vow	Annie West
Duty at What Cost?	Michelle Conder
The Rings That Bind	Michelle Smart
A Marriage Made in Italy	Rebecca Winters
Miracle in Bellaroo Creek	Barbara Hannay
The Courage To Say Yes	Barbara Wallace
Last-Minute Bridesmaid	Nina Harrington

HISTORICAL

Not Just a Governess	Carole Mortimer
A Lady Dares	Bronwyn Scott
Bought for Revenge	Sarah Mallory
To Sin with a Viking	Michelle Willingham
The Black Sheep's Return	Elizabeth Beacon

MEDICAL

NYC Angels: Making the Surgeon Smile	Lynne Marshall
NYC Angels: An Explosive Reunion	Alison Roberts
The Secret in His Heart	Caroline Anderson
The ER's Newest Dad	Janice Lynn
One Night She Would Never Forget	Amy Andrews
When the Cameras Stop Rolling...	Connie Cox

1113 GEN STD LP

ROMANCE

The Dimitrakos Proposition	Lynne Graham
His Temporary Mistress	Cathy Williams
A Man Without Mercy	Miranda Lee
The Flaw in His Diamond	Susan Stephens
Forged in the Desert Heat	Maisey Yates
The Tycoon's Delicious Distraction	Maggie Cox
A Deal with Benefits	Susanna Carr
The Most Expensive Lie of All	Michelle Conder
The Dance Off	Ally Blake
Confessions of a Bad Bridesmaid	Jennifer Rae
The Greek's Tiny Miracle	Rebecca Winters
The Man Behind the Mask	Barbara Wallace
English Girl in New York	Scarlet Wilson
The Final Falcon Says I Do	Lucy Gordon
Mr (Not Quite) Perfect	Jessica Hart
After the Party	Jackie Braun
Her Hard to Resist Husband	Tina Beckett
Mr Right All Along	Jennifer Taylor

MEDICAL

The Rebel Doc Who Stole Her Heart	Susan Carlisle
From Duty to Daddy	Sue MacKay
Changed by His Son's Smile	Robin Gianna
Her Miracle Twins	Margaret Barker

1213 GEN STD HB

Mills & Boon® Large Print

January 2014

ROMANCE

Challenging Dante	Lynne Graham
Captivated by Her Innocence	Kim Lawrence
Lost to the Desert Warrior	Sarah Morgan
His Unexpected Legacy	Chantelle Shaw
Never Say No to a Caffarelli	Melanie Milburne
His Ring Is Not Enough	Maisey Yates
A Reputation to Uphold	Victoria Parker
Bound by a Baby	Kate Hardy
In the Line of Duty	Ami Weaver
Patchwork Family in the Outback	Soraya Lane
The Rebound Guy	Fiona Harper

HISTORICAL

Mistress at Midnight	Sophia James
The Runaway Countess	Amanda McCabe
In the Commodore's Hands	Mary Nichols
Promised to the Crusader	Anne Herries
Beauty and the Baron	Deborah Hale

MEDICAL

Dr Dark and Far-Too Delicious	Carol Marinelli
Secrets of a Career Girl	Carol Marinelli
The Gift of a Child	Sue MacKay
How to Resist a Heartbreaker	Louisa George
A Date with the Ice Princess	Kate Hardy
The Rebel Who Loved Her	Jennifer Taylor

1213 GEN STD LP